T0328515

Sibi's Adventures

in

Alahtene

Sibi's Adventures
in
Alahtene

Mary Fosi Mbantenkhu

SPEARS BOOKS

Denver, Colorado

Spears Books
An Imprint of Spears Media Press LLC
7830 W. Alameda Ave, Suite 103-247
Denver, CO 80226
United States of America

First Published in the United States of America in 2022 by Spears Books
www.spearsmedia.com
info@spearsmedia.com
Information on this title: www.spearsmedia.com/sibis-adventures-in
-alahtene
© 2022 Mary Fosi Mbantenkhu
All rights reserved.

ISBN: 9781942876977 (Paperback)
ISBN: 9781942876984 (eBook)
Also available in Kindle format

Designed and typeset by Spears Media Press LLC
Cover designed by Doh Kambem
Cover art by Bright Toh

Distributed globally by African Books Collective (ABC)
www.africanbookscollective.com

Affectionately dedicated to my Grandmother, Ndih Maria Sirri and to all those loving grandmothers whose stories are untold.

Contents

1

THE JOURNEY

My paternal grandmother, Ndih Maghrebong, must have been about fifty-five years old when she began losing her eyesight. She developed what I came to know later in life as cataract in both eyes. This made her vision blurred. She could recognize people from afar but once objects were very close to her, she would see just a blurry form. Ndih was a determined woman. She wanted to continue doing all the things she had always done despite her visual handicap. I was about five years old when I visited my grandmother for the first time and when I turned six, I told my parents I wanted to live with grandmother or Ndih as she was fondly called.

My father was thrilled by the news, but my mother received it with mixed feelings. "Sibi, how can a kid like you go to stay with grandmother? She needs someone bigger and older who can assist her with house chores and not a kid like you," she said. I started crying and said that I loved Ndih and wanted to live with her. This was 1961, the year I started primary school, a few months after the independence of my country.

I was born in the coastal town of Akoti but my grandma

lived in the savannah village of Alahtene. The journey to Ndih's home in Alahtene started at about 5 a.m. and took a whole day by lorry in the company of my father. Most of the lorries at the busy motor park had flashy colours and names such as *Man no Rest, God's Time is the Best, Money Hard* and so on. My dad and mum chose *God's Time is the Best* for my dad and I. During the trip, I asked my dad why he had chosen *God's time is the Best* and he explained that it was because it surely had God's protection against accidents. Even though a bold notice inside the lorry stated: "No vomiting; No talking to the driver", many passengers still vomited inside the lorry during the long journey. Passengers recounted amusing stories and some of them sounded very frightening. I slept through part of the journey.

The road was very narrow, and no other vehicle came from the opposite direction. I would later learn when I grew up that it was a one-way road and on certain days of the week, vehicles moved only in one direction and on others, they moved in the opposite direction. There were however spots where the vehicles halted and passengers came out of the vehicles to stretch their hurting legs, buy plums, coconuts, roasted plantains, cocoyams, corn, hot koki corn or koki beans and jollof rice.

When we arrived Ndih Maghrebong's home late in the evening, exhausted and hungry after the journey on the dusty and bumpy road, she welcomed us with a broad smile, wide open warm arms and screaming out my name "Sibi, Sibi". She lived with my youngest uncle who may have been about eleven years old at the time. His name was Ajuenekoh. He too was visibly happy to see both of us because my dad, when coming from the coast, usually brought some bread, fried fish, and coconuts. Ajuenekoh's other two siblings were working in the big cities as a steward and overseer respectively.

On arrival, I asked Ndih where her husband was, and she told me he had died some years prior. This, I remembered because my dad had wept bitterly one day and when I had asked why he was crying, he said his dad had passed on to eternity. At the time, I had a very poor understanding of what death meant, so I did not dwell much on the subject. My youngest uncle provided warm water in two separate buckets which we used for a bath after the long journey. Ndih served us dinner and I ate and immediately fell asleep. Although my real name was Nasi, my grandmother fondly called me Sibi.

Ndih had been a very beautiful woman in her youth, well built, fair in complexion and always wore a very beautiful smile on her face. As was the custom of the day in her youth, her body had been beautifully tattooed, her front teeth sharpened by a local dentist, and she would wear a lot of beads (jigida) on her waist just a little bit above her skirts to display her beautiful body. Her neck too always carried some beautiful beads which her own grandmother had handed down to her as an heirloom. The multicoloured beads of her youth were well kept in a wooden box in the barn as part of my inheritance.

She had married my grandfather at about the age of sixteen. My granddad whose nickname was Tah Mohdu was a blacksmith and had many apprentices. He produced all types of farming tools such as hoes, cutlasses, knives, axes, spear heads, dig-axes, guns, pliers, pincers, tapping knives; these he produced using bellows, charcoal fire and iron ore. He was one of the richest persons in a community where everyone else was either a farmer, hunter, builder, or fisherman. He had learned his craft from a very stern craftsman who caned his apprentices.

He had paid a huge bride price to marry my grandmother,

consisting of eight barrels (20 litres each) of palm oil, six jugs of palm wine, two large pigs, five goats, two big bunches of plantains, kola nuts and three brand new pieces of loin cloth for Ndih's sisters. The sum of twenty pounds sterling was also paid. My grandmother said her parents had asked so much bride price so much so that she pitied her prospective husband for providing all those things which cost a lot of money. She said in consequence, her husband had earned the right to demand from any prospective son-in-law, an equal amount of bride price for any of his daughters. Unfortunately, she had no daughter. This meant that her female grandchildren would only get a similar amount of bride price set by my grandfather. However, Ndih's husband was not only happy to pay the bride price, but he also contributed towards a portion of the traditional wedding feast.

My father was the eldest of four boys. Alehnteh was her second, Ayenketeh the third and Ajuenekoh the youngest. Grandmother had lost her two daughters in their infancy. I later learned that the little girls had passed away because of a common childhood disease known as diarrhoea. Ndih explained that when the babies contracted the disease, they vomited and had frequent stools, but she was advised not to give them water. Consequently, the babies became dehydrated and died after a few days. The nearest hospital then was about two days' trek, so most children were never taken to the hospital before their sixth birthday when they could walk a long distance. Ndih's special love for her daughters was soon transferred to me, her first granddaughter. She and I had a special bond, and every villager who saw me always remarked about the close resemblance between my grandmother and me.

2

ALAHBUKUM AND ALAHTENE

The kingdom of Alahbukum is composed of more than forty villages. It is one of the most powerful kingdoms in the northern side of the English-speaking part of Meroonca. The dynasty has existed for over six hundred years. It has one of the richest cultures south of the Sahara. The inhabitants were originally warriors who came from another country (possibly Piatheo), conquering other indigenous peoples and making them pay allegiance to their king and his nobles. The king who reigned over Alahbukum when my grandmother was a young girl was called *Cover of the Earth* because his kingdom covered a surface area which one could not travel across in a week on foot. He was a very tall and heavily built man. *Cover of the Earth* had succeeded as king his own father known as *Conqueror of the World*.

He had resisted the German colonial occupation vigorously so much so that the Germans had to go through another conquered neighbouring kingdom's king who betrayed *Cover of the Earth* by sending him a messenger who pretended that he was bringing some guests to visit him. When the German soldiers who came as friends reached the Palace of Alabukum and saw the magnificent structures there - the individual houses of the king's wives built around the palace in an oval form, the various parts of the palace, the place under the Everlasting Plum tree, the Palace Sacred House (Achume Nfor) where kings were enthroned and where they went "Missing" (because it was believed that kings of Alahbukum never died but simply disappeared from the face of the earth); the outer palace reception hall, the inner courtyard; the princes' quarters, the royal sacred forest among others), the Germans were astounded by the kingdom's level of development. They captured the king who had welcomed them as guests and later took him to a coastal town and he was later transferred to an Island called Fernando Po. One of his wives was also taken into captivity with the king to this distant foreign land where they lived without aides, completely isolated and cut off from the rest of the world. The king was made to execute menial jobs like felling trees, splitting firewood with axes and bathing by himself as punishment for resisting German colonial rule. He was about forty-five years old when he was sent on exile by his captors.

When the people of Alahbukum later learned of the king's capture and eventual transfer to a foreign land, some of the most vulnerable ones committed suicide and the rest of the population went into mourning for an undetermined period. Men went about with their hair and beards unshaven for the whole time the king was under captivity; women had to shave their hair completely, wore only skirts with their breast left bare, no beads on their necks or waists and young men wore some form of underpants, (*ngwasie*), the King's Annual Dance was suspended; many nobles changed their diet from eating *achu* with yellow soup to black soup; these acts were meant to express their pain for the "loss" of their king. The darkest moment came when rumours went around that the king had died in captivity.

When the Germans saw the resolute manner with which the people of Alahbukum mourned their king (supposedly dead), they decided to bring back the captured king after a year's detention, which seemed like four years to the population. The German colonisers concluded a deal with *Mfor, Cover of the Earth* and his nobles – which stipulated that they would never again attack the occupiers. During the signing of the treaty, *Cover of the Earth* who could neither read nor write the German language was given a bird's feather with black ink on it to cross two crooked lines on the paper as a sign of his signature. Word of the signing of the treaty reached all the villages of the kingdom and the men had their hair and beards shaved after a year; women covered their naked breasts with pieces of new cloth tied to their back and once again, allowed their hair to grow; and young men wore shirts made from jute bags commonly called *mukuta* bags.

The population that gathered at the palace and all its surroundings during the occasion sang the anthem known as *mban* (kids, adults, old men, and women chanted the hymn); an anthem so solemn to listen to, it raises goose bumps on every listener. Immediately after the anthem, one of the king's wives, in a high shrieking voice, lavished praises on the king - *a tree with many thorns, the baobab tree on which all types of animals and insects hide; the one who when he passes, even cocks acknowledge his presence by crowing; the son of the formidable kwifor; the link between the ancestors and the living,* etc. When she was done, the king cleared his throat and began to speak. He addressed his subjects in the local language, thanked them for standing strong before the enemy, and insisted that the Germans had lost the war which they had acknowledged by negotiating to pay damages by building and roofing the entire palace, including the promise to support the operation of a museum. That his release was testimony that no other kingdom can ever "cover" the earth of Alahbukum. He thanked his ancestors for protecting him thus far, and invited the entire population to celebrate by eating, drinking and firing their guns. Immediately, several notables danced to one direction and fired their Dane guns in the air to the utmost surprise of the Germans who were at the ceremonial ground.

Consequently, there was feasting and celebrations for several days throughout the kingdom. The Germans compensated the king for depriving him of his liberty by building a storey building in the palace and roofing all the palace houses that belonged to the one hundred wives with red brick tiles. They also taught the local crafts men how to produce the red brick tiles. The palace storey building has more than eighty-five steps leading into that section of the palace. The palace has now become a world cultural heritage site according to UNESCO classification. The king however kept all the captured guns and headgear the Germans wore during the war against his people. These are currently displayed in the palace museum.

Alahtene was one of the many villages under the rule of King *Cover of the Earth*. *Cover of the Earth* who had an expansionist vision for his kingdom usually ordered the nobles, princes and the peasants to go to distant fertile areas and bring home game, do farming and fishing to feed the ever-growing population of the king's palace. This village was initially a great "track" linking Alabuhkum and Alahbugweh. Another track linked Alahbechonge and connected Alahtene to Aghahsaah.

It was therefore a crossroads village. Alahtene village started with farmhouses where the nobles and princes would stay for a short while, farm crops and domesticate animals like goats, fowls, pigs, etc., hunted and fished, dried their harvest and then transported these items back to the central villages in Alahbukum (with a good portion usually sent to the king). Gradually, as the harvest became abundant and transportation became a major challenge, people began to build permanent homes in Alahtene. My grandparents were among the founding fathers of Alahtene in the kingdom of Alahbukum.

Ndih's House

My grandmother's house was located around the Alahtene village market square where the main intersection leads to four different directions. It was in a compound of two houses, one of which belonged to my father. His house comprised a parlour and two bedrooms. Important guests were received at my father's house when he was around. The house was constantly locked as he was gone most of the time. My grandmother's house was about a hundred yards from my father's. It comprised a large kitchen with a small window and an attached room to its left which belonged to uncle Ajeunekoh. Ndih's kitchen-like room had four bamboo beds installed around the four walls of the house with a fireside in the middle of the room. There was a barn under the ceiling; a long type of bamboo cabin from one side of the width of the room to the other which served as a cupboard for storing most kitchen essentials; it was called *abangue* or the long shelf. Ndih's house was so beautiful to look at, especially the artistic elements its builders had applied during its construction. Sticks of varying sizes were used, firmly driven into the ground, tied to each other, then mud bricks were used in the front part with additional poles to support the roof that was thatched with grass. The clay used to plaster the inside was dark, but it had blackened due to smoke and the heat from the fireside. The room had a very small window where some of the smoke from the fireside occasionally found an outlet. The window was normally shut for most of the year. The enclosed nature of the room preserved heat which facilitated the drying of foodstuff preserved in the ceiling. Even though the room was generally smoky, some of it went out through the doorway and the thatched roof. Both my father's and grandmother's houses had bamboo roofs thatched with a special type of grass.

Although there were four beds inside grandmother's house, I still shared Ndih's bed in order to keep myself warm. Additional sources of heat included the fireside in the middle of the house and a thick blanket that always smelled of smoke. Another reason I shared Ndih's bed was due to fright. Many of the stories told in the evenings were often frightful, consisting of witches, ghosts and aliens, wild animals like lions and large snakes which usually swallowed their victims; so I could not dare sleep alone for fear of being eaten up at night by the deadly beasts or ghosts in the stories. When Ndih ran out of firewood at night, she would quickly remove some of the bamboos from the bed's platform to keep the fire glowing. The bed was covered with a mat made with raffia fibre to soften the hard bamboo platform. Ndih's removal of the bamboos from the platform often created large gap in the bed. Since I hardly slept in my bed, I would often curl up behind Ndih and quickly fall asleep but when I stretched myself or rolled over, I would slip between the big gaps and land directly on the floor. Ndih would call for me to get up from the cold dirt floor back into bed but as a deep sleeper, she would have to shout my name "Sibi" several times. I would jump to my feet, startled, and hurriedly climb back to the bamboo bed. Most weekends, the other beds were also occupied by other kids who came to partake in our storytelling or enjoy other activities. Many of them usually fell asleep during the storytelling sessions. Some were picked up by their parents late at night while others, if they were relatives, were just left there to sleep till morning. Many of the children who spent the night at Ndih's place rose early in the morning, picked the fallen ripe fruits such as pears, plums or mangoes (depending on their season) and munched them on their way back to their parents' home.

Ndih's compound had many fruit trees including pear and mango trees, orange, plum, palm, guava and pawpaw trees. Sugar cane was also widely planted. All the fruit trees produced very juicy fruits according to their season. I enjoyed all the fruits and Ndih used to poke fun at me that I overate the fruits like a bird. Ndih also planted coffee trees in one section of the compound which produced an abundance of beans. When the coffee trees matured, they would first produce beautiful white flowers which were eventually replaced by the coffee beans. At first, they would appear as green seeds and with time, became red and sweet when they ripened. Because we enjoyed sucking and keeping them in our mouths for long, Ndih advised my friends and I to be careful not to swallow them. The harvested coffee beans were usually conserved in large baskets or containers to ferment, then washed and sun dried. Buyers often came around during the coffee harvesting season to buy and it was measured in kilograms. This was one of Ndih's main sources of income. We used to wonder what the buyers did with the dried coffee beans until we learned later in school that coffee was a main cash crop of my country and that the beans were in high demand as a beverage all over the world.

So many birds perched or spent the night at Ndih's premises including bats. Some of the birds we frequently saw at Ndih's compound included songbirds, weaver birds, owls, kites, hawks, bush fowls, and woodpeckers. Early birds would chirp every morning and served as timekeepers that woke Ndih up. As soon as she woke up, she would start to roast either sweet potatoes, yams, plantains or cocoyams and when I woke up, she would serve me one of these crunchy meals as breakfast. I would eat before brushing my teeth with a chewing stick. Each time my father sent us toothpaste, I would invite my friends over and we'll jointly eat the paste as if it were candy. Subsequently, I would brush my teeth without toothpaste. Little did we know how dangerous toothpaste is. Just like Ndih and the other villagers, I resorted to using a chewing stick to brush my teeth every morning.

My father would also send a packet of sugar to Ndih which we consumed by putting it in our tea or morning pap (corn powder porridge). When we ran out of sugar, we would use the wild honey my uncle harvested. In the absence of either sugar or honey, we would sprinkle a bit of salt into our pap to make it tasteful.

Ndih could tell the time depending on which bird made what sound and if you had a clock to crosscheck, you would be amazed by her accuracy. Certain foods required that Ndih should begin cooking them as early as four o'clock in the morning such as beans or colocasia. Ndih depended on the chirping of specific birds or a cock's crow to wake up early and begin cooking. As for me, as soon as I curled into bed, I would hardly hear a cock's crow or a bird's chirp. Some of my earliest memories included women who came by early in the morning to see Ndih and they would complain about owls that hooted at night or cats that meowed all night in their compounds. These nocturnal noises were considered bad omen in Alahtene. Ndih would reassure the worried women, telling them that perhaps the "witches" were just passing by on their way to some other place and that no bad news would come their way.

Many barefooted children with tattered clothes and runny noses also visited Ndih's compound supposedly to play with me although their real intent was to eat some of the fruits. They always ended up asking for fruits and Ndih would grant them permission to harvest as much fruits as they wanted. She would exclaim to herself: "how did I know I was going to have so many children who could eat all these fruits that God has blessed me with?"

The smoke in Ndih's house was usually unbearable especially after eating her hot spicy pepper soup. The pepper soup induced mucus from one's nostrils while the smoke produced tear drops from one's eyes simultaneously. I once quizzed Ndih why she cooked, ate and slept in her kitchen, and she responded that it was the way her parents had raised her. The smoke that accumulated each day at Ndih's kitchen and house seemed too unfriendly for a young newcomer's eyes. It took me a long time to get accustomed to Ndih's smoky kitchen. I therefore promised Ndih that when I grow up, I would build her a good house with a kitchen separated from her bedroom. She was apparently pleased with the idea but feared that such a house may be too cold. *La casa de ma Mieula* is a fulfilment of that promise.

Ndih's compound was a few yards from the village market. Market days (commonly known as *Mbindoh*) were always

interesting for a variety of reasons; first because of the colourful clothes worn by both men and women, the types of
goods sold, then the noisy bee-like chatter of human voices
and lastly, the outburst of fighting that usually took place late in
the afternoons after some of the market attendees were drunk
from drinking palm/raffia wine, corn beer, *akwacha* or *smulgri*. The market was interesting also because one would find
people from all backgrounds, including mad persons whose
behaviours often appeared strange.

3

NDIH MAGHREBONG'S NEIGHBOURS

My grandmother's house was surrounded by four neigh-bours. The compound on the left belonged to Tah Ghekembow who had a wife and four children. His mother lived in his compound with two of her sons and four grand-children. His wife's nephew also lived with them. It was a compound of at least thirteen people during normal times and about twenty during holidays. I envied their numbers because at Ndih's house, we were only three of us. When I enquired from one of the grandchildren who was my age mate on the whereabouts of her biological mother, she told me sadly that she had died. Her father had consequently remarried, and her new stepmother wasn't treating her well. That's how she had ended up living with their grandmother. This was the second time I heard about someone's death, the first having been my paternal grandfather.

Tah Ghekembow was a very huge man and with very large hands. He always played tricks on children when they were eating boiled groundnuts. He would ask a kid if he could get some of their groundnuts from their baskets. With the child's permission, he would place his large hands into the basket and empty almost all the groundnuts. This gesture always provoked sadness and tears as no child expected to lose almost all their groundnut so suddenly.

A typical characteristic of children from Tah Ghekembow's compound was that they enjoyed bullying other kids. They also had the habit of calling other children's father's names without the customary honorific, Tah, which is the equivalent of Mr. in English. This was sufficient reason to provoke a fight in those days. Engaging in a fight with one of the kids in that compound also meant one should be ready to fight all the kids in that compound. It was a well-known fact that the kids did not hesitate to join a fight against anyone in support of their kin, irrespective of who or what had originally provoked the fight. That is how they earned the nickname, "United Team of Alahtene Fighters".

Their grandmother had married at a young age to a husband in a different ethnic group where she bore many children. Her husband had died in middle age and her in-laws no longer wanted her to live in the land because she was considered a foreigner. However, she was now very fluent in her husband's mother tongue and tended to mix it with *Befue* – our language. She was almost a stranger to her own culture when she eventually returned to Alahtene and many local kids thought she was a foreigner. She loved and protected her orphaned grandchildren. It was believed that she and only a few close friends knew what had led her grandchildren to be orphaned at such a tender age.

The neighbour to the right was Tah Muwungho. He had a wife, five children and two other relatives who lived with them. Like my father, he was away from home most of the time. His wife was also much younger than Ndih Maghrebong. As a carpenter, he specialised in roofing people's houses in the city and was the only person in all of Alahtene with a house that had corrugated iron roofing. Mischievous boys passing by often threw stones on his roof and enjoyed hearing the sound it produced. They would take off when the man's wife came out to see for herself who the mischievous persons were. Somehow, it seems the children enjoyed the curses she directed at them.

I quickly befriended his first daughter on our way to fetch water from the stream the day after my arrival. We played together and learned how to climb trees to pluck fruits such as pears, mangoes, guavas, oranges and plums. As tree climbing was a mainly male activity, we eventually earned the name of tomboys. We also fetched firewood together.

The neighbour directly behind Ndih's compound was called Tah Nujala. He was an ex-soldier, who in other parts of the world, would have been hailed as a national hero but in Alahtene, he was considered a wizard because he had killed so many people in many battles in strange lands but never received a bullet on his body. His grandson and all the village kids loved him so much because he told them interesting stories of far-off lands which we imagined existed in heaven only.

The other neighbour close to the stream on the right was called Tah Tegha. He was a very calm man and spoke very little. He lived with his wife, six children and two other young female relatives who were identical twins. It was so difficult for me to distinguish the twins, so I often fumbled their names, and they would laugh at me, saying how could a young coastal girl like myself not distinguish them? I always felt so miserable and ended up asking one of my friends to tell me how to distinguish them. She advised that I must crack a joke each time I met them and when they laughed, I would distinguish the one with a dimple. My jokes hardly yielded the expected results, so I continued mixing up their names. The neighbour's oldest daughter also became my friend. Her father had a very wild hunting dog feared by everyone in the neighbourhood. However, once the dog became familiar with me, I could gain access to their compound without the dog barking or trying to scare me off.

4

THE VILLAGE HEAD

The village head was a sub-chief. He was known as Tanekruh Akolui. He was one of the four earliest young men who courageously trekked from Alahtene for over a week in search of greener pastures to the coastal town where I was born. My father was one of the four and they had survived the tedious journey by eating a mixture of fried corn with roasted ground-nuts and ripe bananas. The village head was a robust man with great energy and his face was always beaming with a smile. During the great trek to the coast, he had served as the leader of the team and confronted anyone who sought to bully his mates. They were on their way to find work in the newly created German-owned giant banana and rubber plantations. They were all tall, hardworking, and lively teenagers then. Upon their arrival in the coast, they had to bribe their way into new jobs (popularly called *chappeers* and *waterboy* respectively) by giving each, a live cock to the supervisor. Even though the pay was mean, they saved their hard-earned money with the intention to return home to build a house and pay the bride price for a new wife.

The village head kept a frugal life and neither drank corn beer nor *smulgri* like some of his peers. Upon his return home to Alahtene, he was considered very rich by village standards. He built six houses in his compound and one of them was roofed with corrugated iron sheets.

He had five wives then and many children. It was rumoured that he did not even recognize many of his own children or knew their names. His children who belonged to various age groups would greet him "Tahgha" which means daddy in English, and he would respond: "whose son/daughter are you?" The child would usually respond "am I not your child born by X mother?" Then he would smile broadly and say, "Am I not trying? Does the king know the names of most of his own children? Even in this village, many parents do not recognize their own children", he would say! His real name was Ajueteyoure.

He was also the head of the village council of elders (*Ndah Butah*), which was composed of eight members. The figure eight also represented the number of days of the week in Alahbukum (*Njwi'la'a, Mbi'ndoo, Mumitaa, Mitaniba'a, Nko'ofikuu, Ntooba'li, Yika, Yijong*). These men participated in resolving land disputes, debt collection, judging cases of theft, fights, boundary disputes between neighbours, transmission of instructions or information from the king to the villagers, proposing villagers to be knighted by the king, etc. When issues involved only women, they convened the Women Elders among whom my grandmother was a member. However, she did not to like to participate in these meetings because the village head would intervene to seek favours on behalf of certain persons. The village councillors were men with large protruding stomachs. It was an open secret that before each case was heard, both the plaintiff and the defendant would each bring a goat, food and drinks. It was also required that every bereaved family, prior to the burial of the deceased person (if she/he hailed from the village), should present to the councillors, a big pig, twenty-four bundles of achu, three roasted chickens, several jugs (20 litres each) of palm or raffia wine and two crates of *smulgri* (beer smuggled from the neighbouring country to the East). Eventually, Ndih became fed up with the man's constant obstruction of justice as he came to see Ndih privately to pervert justice by telling her what to do when confronted with female cases. Many villagers would shake their heads in shock and disgust when they recounted the councillors' long history of perverting justice. Villagers frequently commented that except for the female elders, almost all the male councillors would die with their eyes open and their bellies swollen, a sign that underscored the view that the deceased had committed many atrocities during his/her lifetime. Others said that upon death, the spirit of the corrupt village councillors would be restless because they would still be seeking means to claim their uncollected bribes.

One of the councillors could not dare talk in public because the youth were always ready to boo him. Tah Maki, the notorious councillor, was reported to have caught a live chicken that belonged to someone else, twisted the poor bird's neck and hid it in his handbag. This incident reportedly took place not far from a school field where young children were playing a football match. He had no idea that the kids in the playground had seen him commit the act and that they had alerted the rest of the crowd. Suddenly, the football match stopped; the players and spectators ran up to him and challenged him to show the content of his handbag. The councillor resisted the children's request stating that kids were not competent to search an elder's bag. So, all the kids followed him and chanted this song:

What a thief of a councillor, so all the fowls missing every day in this village are stolen by you. The chicken is in your bag, open the bag and let us inspect it now. Thief, highway robber, who sits in the village council pretending to judge people.

As the crowd of young angry people who followed him grew bigger and bigger, he was fortunate to see one of his fellow councillors approaching from the opposite direction, who sought to know why a crowd of children was following him. Maki responded: "take this handbag that I'm carrying, look inside with the eyes of an old man and see whether there is any chicken inside. These kids are accusing me of being a thief. Just check the contents of my bag and see for yourself whether there is a chicken inside." The other councillor took the bag, held it close to his chest and pretended to inspect its contents. After inspecting the bag, he said to the children "my children, where is the chicken you guys are talking about? This bag has no such thing in it."

He handed the bag to his friend and said "take your bag and go your way. I think these kids were dreaming especially as the sun is so hot! Children, go home to your parents and never accuse an old man of stealing unless you have the proof." Although the children dispersed, many of them swore that they had seen the accused councillor twist the neck of a life chicken and put it in his handbag. Some of the kids believed the man had magically made the chicken disappear from his bag. The story spread around the whole village that very evening as each child recounted it to their parents. Their parents in turn discussed the matter in the farms, in *njangi* houses and at every drinking spot. It became public talk but the older boys in the village swore that they would never allow that councillor to talk in public.

One of village head's daughters who belonged to my age group easily became my friend. She told me that she admired me because I wore shoes to church service and wished she too could own a pair of shoes. This statement surprised me because I had thought all along that the village kids of my age did not like to wear shoes.

The head of the village council was a grandson of the king and was thus considered a link between royal blood and commoners although he took delight in being called prince (*Moo*). His actions and speech could be deceptive because he always sought to benefit from both the royal family and commoners. He owned a substantial amount of land in Alahtene and frequently carried several gifts on his bicycle to the palace

After two weeks in the village, my dad told Ndih he had to return to his job because he had taken a short vacation to accompany me on the trip. He had indeed enjoyed his short vacation, having spent some time with the village head and their two other friends as they reminisced about their trek to the coast. Ndih was so delighted and grateful for his stay. At the time, my dad worked as a driver for one of the colonial officers. He wore khaki shorts and a khaki long sleeve shirt when going to work. His boss wore a white khaki short and white long sleeve shirt as well as a white pith hat. He also wore spectacles. My father regularly had a haircut with a decorative line made on the left side of his head - a very popular style in those days. He was very tall and lanky and had inherited his handsome looks and smile from his mother. As he left, he advised me to be a very good girl to his mother, which I followed as best as I could.

A few months later, dad returned to the village to work on the construction of a new road that would link the village to the city. Upon hearing the noise produced by the heavy-duty truck, villagers, both young, old and crippled, men and women rushed out of their houses and bars to the main street with tree branches in their hands, waving joyously and praising the driver. I too rushed to the scene to see what was happening. To my surprise, everyone was cheering at my dad for being the first person to drive such a vehicle through what was once a foot path. The next week, all the villagers went out to dig the road with spades, hoes, axes and cutlasses. The new road, about eight miles long dissected through hills, streams and valleys.

5

A COMMUNITY GRINDING MILL

Ndih Maghrebong had a giant grinding stone in her compound which was used for grinding various food items: roasted dry corn (for fufu and pap), groundnuts and egusi (for pudding) and general food seasoning. Corn fufu was one of the staples besides achu. The latter was prepared from pounded Colocasia and eaten with yellow soup, made with heated palm oil, *niki* or alkaline stone, cooked cow skin, boiled eggplant, mushroom and a blend of seven local spices: *feloh, sop, kinge, aloh, mbahcheh, akuuh* and *neghe.* An alternative sauce known as black soup was prepared with ground roasted elephant grass stocks, ground boiled dried Colocasia leaves called *ambaha;* tadpoles and *feloh.* Hot yellow or red pepper was never absent in any of the dishes. Corn fufu was often eaten with various types of sauteed vegetables such as huckleberries, cow pea leaves, bitter herbs (commonly known as bitter leaves), okra, pumpkin leaves cooked with fresh boiled groundnut paste; amaranth (commonly referred to as green); egusi soup, etc. Of these vegetables, huckleberry was the most popular, underscored by the popular saying that fufu corn is the husband to njama-njama (huckleberries). Every item that needed to be ground was done on Ndih's giant grinding stone, which served as the village's big grinding mill.

Many older boys came in most evenings and demonstrated their strength by grinding roasted corn into corn powder on the large grinding stone. Sometimes, villagers would ground fresh corn which was used to prepare koki corn, fresh beans for koki beans and fresh corn for pap. The young men's labour usually earned them a few coins. These same boys usually ground Ndih's own food items for free because she owned the stone.

One day, a team of white missionaries visited the village on a fact-finding mission with the goal of improving the nutritional needs of the population. They heard about Ndih's giant grinding stone and paid an impromptu visit to the compound and saw for themselves the amount of time put into the process of grinding corn on stone. Photographs of Ndih's grinding stone were snapped including the throng of barefooted happy, chatty children who were awaiting their turn to grind their corn. The children were very excited to be photographed even though they would never see the pictures. After a few months, the missionaries brought back as a gift in a vehicle, a brand-new mechanical corn mill, much to the delight of the population.

The village head readily allocated a piece of land where the community built a house to contain the equipment. An installation ceremony took place amidst dancing, singing and speeches. Baskets of assorted fruits were given as gifts to the missionaries as well as flowers from the lone primary school's garden. Many villagers brought dried corn (unroasted) to be ground at the mill. The machine had two handles and required two individuals to run them. The arrival of the machine truly transformed the lives of the villagers because it replaced Ndih's giant grinding stone. However, the population's happiness was short-lived. Less than two years after its installation, the population awoke one early morning, and discovered that the corn mill had been stolen at night. Doors to the building that housed the machine had been smashed opened by men of the underworld and the equipment uprooted from where it had been firmly implanted. Villagers wept profusely for this huge loss, as they saw the theft of their machine as an attempt to stall their development.

Since the population had become accustomed to the mechanical corn mill and had abandoned Ndih's grinding stone, women and young people resumed carrying bags of corn on their heads to be milled in town. Villagers who were considered rich and could afford bicycles, usually rode to town carrying bags of corn on their bicycles to be milled. On their way back, they would ride their bicycles downhill and if children were playing on the main road, the riders would shout out, "give way because I don't have a bell on my bike." The older boys would yell back at the rider saying, "sell your bike and buy yourself a bell!" As a kid, this always sounded funny to me. What on earth would the person do with a bell without a bicycle? I thought to myself.

Ndih's giant grinding stone had contributed a lot to alleviating the suffering of Alahtene's people. I used to wonder about Ndih and her husband's ingenuity in procuring and then shaping such a stone into a grinding instrument. How did they carry it to the spot where it lay? How did they shape it? What great technicians my grandparents were!

A couple of years following the theft of the grinding machine, some young people discovered an old grinding machine in a nearby village and reported it to the village council, assuming it was the stolen machine. An investigation was made which established that the discovered machine was a much older, abandoned machine.

6

THE VILLAGE MARKET

The village market was just a few yards away from Ndih's house. It was in fact built on land that Ndih and her husband had donated to the village. Before my grandparents donated that piece of land, villagers sold their products by the main roadside. As the population grew bigger and bigger, the crowd of sellers and buyers would block the road, making it difficult for bike riders and the few vehicles that plied the road. The village head allocated a piece of land for the market a couple of kilometres from the village centre, but villagers rejected the offer. That's how my grandparents ended up donating a portion of their land for the village market. In exchange, they were offered the land rejected by the villagers which they used as one of their garden plots. Villagers wasted no time in constructing stalls around the new market. Villagers also contributed to build a latrine with three separate rooms, one for men, another for women and the third for children. The market had a sanitary inspector sent by the king of Alahbukum whose job was to inspect everything especially food stuff on sale. Those that he found unfit for human consumption were thrown away. More often than not, these items included palm oil, garri and meat.

On market days, business started early, and the noise grew louder with the population's increase. When the market was at its height, the noise sounded like a huge swamp of bees. People often wore very colourful clothes to the market. One could easily distinguish couples because they wore the same fabric. A wife would have a colourful dress or wrapper while her husband would have either his trouser or jumper shirt sewn from the same fabric. Other men wore the local attire *atoghu*, colourfully woven with black, red, yellow and sometimes green threads, with a cap and occasionally a feather on it. The feather indicated that its wearer had been recognised or knighted by the king for some meritorious act.

The market was the preferred location for transmitting information from the king's palace by the town crier. He would wait for the market to reach its full capacity before blowing the giant buffalo horn to attract the population's attention. This normally took a short while and eventually, the people stopped chattering and turned their attention to the messengers. Then the king's messengers would communicate the information. Instructions communicated from the monarch usually concerned the dates for contributing raffia palm wine, hunting game for the king, farming his fields, building a bridge over a certain stream or river in the kingdom, or some other kind of community activity.

Many people came to the market to sell, buy, drink, get news about friends and relatives and for some, to provoke a fight. The butchers sold fresh meat, some women sold palm oil, several types of food crops - puff puff, cooked foods like koki corn, koki beans, cooked yams, garri, varieties of spices;

green plantains, fruits, vegetables, smoked bush meat, dried fish, clothes, akwacha and smulgri. Men usually sold goats, pigs, fowls, fried termites, local medicinal ingredients and raffia/palm wine. Many of them ended up squandering their money on smulgri from the neighbouring countries of Meroonca and Reigania.

Beggars and mad people also attended the market. There was a notorious blind beggar called "Troubleman". His arrival was always a crowd pulling event because he sang a variety of inspirational songs that recounted his life story and what had caused his blindness at the prime of his life. He always sang songs that carried important life lessons such as this: *that nobody ever waits for trouble (misfortune), but that trouble can find you even if you are minding your business.* His songs were so soul touching that almost everybody gave him a coin. Mr. Troubleman had a son, possibly about my age who used to dance to his father's songs and assisted in collecting the coins spectators and sympathisers threw on the ground as alms for them. After Mr. Troubleman departed (since he came from a distant village), we the village kids would perform and dance to his songs. Ndih did not like listening to me sing such songs because she thought they sounded like an invitation for trouble (ill-luck).

Some people who were known troublemakers usually came to the market to stir a fight. Such fights, started by two drunk quarrelsome individuals, usually ended in a public fight because once a person's friend or relative was given a solid blow even in error, someone would join the fight to support either kin or friend. People were usually drunk before the fight and this was the most interesting part because once a drunken person was given a blow, he immediately staggered and fell to the

ground to the utmost anger of his family members or friends
who quickly found a valid reason to join the fight to defend
him. By the time the brawl ended, many people would be on
the ground shouting "I'm dead, I'm dead". This was one of the
moments I most dreaded although no one ever died during
these brawls at the market. Nevertheless, the fighters seemed
to enjoy it because its origin was often unpredictable, and the
fights seemed to entertain us as children.

Traders came from far and wide to buy beef and food stuff
from the Alahtene market to resell them in city markets. One
day, as villagers enjoyed themselves in the market drinking local
corn beer, akwacha, smulgri beer and dancing in bars while
others plotted to stir a fight, a big lorry suddenly arrived at the
market entrance. Uniform officers jumped out of it and dispersed in all directions in the market. Those who sold smulgri
thought the officers with red caps had come to arrest them, so
they began to hide the smuggled beers in large *mukuta* bags
underneath benches in their bars. Contrary to what the population expected, the law enforcement officials began to arrest
all the men in the market and ordered them to show their tax
payment receipts. Many of the men did not go about with their
poll tax payment receipts and were thus arrested and carried
off to the police station in the city, about ten miles away. Many
people in Alahtene thought the frequent brawls on market days
had prompted the law enforcement officers' visit.

The women whose husbands, sons, brothers and friends
had been arrested began to wail as it was customary at the
funeral of a beloved person. They fell with their faces flat on
the ground, rolled on the dusty floor in their colourful dresses,
and declared they were finished; that life for them and their
children had ended because their husbands or brothers had

been arrested by the police for imprisonment. People helped them to their feet and comforted them, telling them that they will do everything to bail out the detainees. Latecomers to the market heard the news of the arrest and hid themselves in the bushes for two days in fear that the officers would return for further arrests.

The next morning, many women came to Ndih to borrow money. They would use it to bail out, bribe the officers or settle unpaid taxes for their loved ones. When the men were eventually liberated, they returned to the village and recounted the cruel treatment they had received from their jailers. It frightened the entire population. From that day, very few men attended the village market for fear of *Jahs* – the term villagers had coined for the gendarmes with red caps who arrested men who had not paid their poll tax. This was also the last year a group public fight took place in Alahtene market.

A year earlier, this same market had been the venue of bubbling political activities. The British colonial masters had become fed up with colonisation and wanted to relinquish power without actually granting the territory independence. They had hastily concocted a plan by means of a referendum that would enable the territory to gain self-rule by joining another independent country to its left or joining the one on its right. Several political parties aspiring to win votes for the so-called independence elections, held their political rallies at Alahtene Market. All the Parties had their respective political colours, symbols and flags. The most interesting one was known as "Nkom Akehe" meaning "the Cock's Ballot Box" formed by a local hero. It stood for the country to gain its independence by joining the neighbouring country to the west. In preparation for the event, a song was composed by Alahtene villagers to support their local hero Tah Nkom-Akehe. The song called on everyone to vote only for the Cock's Ballot Box which was going to provide free education to all the population, free medical care for all, good roads linking Alahteneh to any part of the world; no payment of poll taxes for men; construction of modern bridges to replace the wooden bridges in Alahtene, buying of coffee at ten times the current market price… Every villager felt thrilled by these promises. They all sang and danced the *Nkom-Akehe* song because as long as the world rotated, the cock will always crow early in the morning! Other political parties' representatives also came to the market to win the minds and votes of the naive inhabitants of Alahtene by making utopian promises. The villagers all came out each time campaign caravans were passing by. The political aspirants tried to convince the villagers how they were somehow related to them in one way or the other. Each politician recounted that they had family who lived in Alahtene and that Alahtene was the future United States of Alahbukum. Many villagers were thrilled by the vain promises and some started wondering whether voting for their local hero was really worth the pain or the wisest choice. At night when the political rallies ended, secret meetings were held by the confused villagers to discuss politics and their common position.   Some of the campaigners usually came at nightfall to request Ndih to use her influence to persuade the women to vote for such and such a party.

Nevertheless, as the saying goes, blood is thicker than water – and when the polls opened, almost all of Alahtene's population voted for Nkom Akehe. Unfortunately for the inhabitants of Alahtene, their local hero's party did not win in the elections as they wanted the country to gain independence by joining a hugely populated country found on the west of Meroonca with the intention of becoming a fully-fledged country a few years later. Independence by joining the country to the East, declared a year later, meant very little or nothing to the population of Alahtene as long as their hero did not win the elections. They predicted that most of the population had taken a regrettable decision and regretted the fact that if their hero had won, Alahtene would have been transformed into an earthly paradise. So, when people were arrested from the same market a year later, the population cursed the day some voters were tricked to cast their votes in favour of joining the country on the east.

Members of that political party reminded villagers in bars at the market that their local party had predicted the maltreatment to be expected if the population voted the other way. They reminded anyone who wanted to hear that the king of Alahbukum had during the time of the so-called elections known as the plebiscite warned everybody that joining the densely populated country to the west was like drowning in the deep sea while also joining the other country on the east was like jumping into a furnace of fire! They even quoted the then United Nations Secretary General Dag Hammarskjold who had stated that joining the country to the East was like forcing a balloon under the sea and that one day it will come out.

They said if the foolish majority had listened to them, then this type of shabby treatment would not have been meted on free citizens of an independent country. Many people promised to boycott the smulgri beer from that country as a show of their discontent with the government to the east. They started plans to create their own brewery in Alahtene. They suggested that the production of *nkang* and other local beers would be transformed into breweries. One evening, many frightened women came to see grandmother to brainstorm on what the consequences would be for their own nkang or akwacha private businesses should a new local brewery be created.

7

NDIH MAGHREBONG'S THREE FRIENDS

Ndih Maghrebong had three friends, Mah Ngwebangie, Mah Ngwebancho and Mah Mabifor. They usually met on market days at Ndih's place, smoked their tobacco pipes together and ate some local foods which each of them brought, drank some sweet palm wine or sweet corn beer. Incidentally, three of the four women were widows. Mah Ngwebangie was a neighbour whose house was on the left side of Ndih's. She lived with her son and several grandchildren. She had been married during her youth to a foreigner from another ethnic group and at the death of her husband, she had returned to Alahtene to her parents' compound. Her husband's brothers had allegedly expelled her from their marital home after her husband's demise, thereby taking over that property as their own. She and her young children had no power to protest this injustice. When she returned to Alahtene after several years spent in her husband's homeland, she had the tendency to ·mix up two languages - that of her late husband's and her own mother tongue. Many kids who heard her talk thought she was a foreigner and thus earned the nickname "Ndih the foreigner."

Mah Ngwebancho was the neighbour directly behind Ndih's house. She lived with her husband, a son and a grandson who was my uncle, Ajuenekoh's age mate. She was the only one with a surviving husband amongst the four old ladies. However, she was away from her home most of the time, leaving her husband Tah Nujala (a former German soldier) and her grandson alone. Her son had a farmhouse in a certain village where the main river had a lot of fish and plenty of game in the surrounding forest. He frequently lived in the farmhouse during which he fished and hunted. Her grandson, Newhenenchu was one of her daughters' first son. He and Ajuenekoh were very close friends. They would hunt, fish and gather termites after school or during the holidays. They usually cooked food and game for Tah Nujala, the boy's grandfather. The latter had returned from World War I where he had fought as a real patriot on the side of his colonial masters, the Germans.

He had visited many foreign countries as a young soldier. Most of the kids in Alahtene loved him because he told them amusing and strange stories of his adventures in far off lands. He usually started his stories by recounting how he entered ships, wearing German soldiers' uniforms, boots, helmet and backpack, learning the German language, eating foreign foods, arriving on land after spending several weeks on the high seas, swimming in the sea with his gun lifted up in the sky to reach dry shores when the ships arrived their destination. Immediately he and his comrades in arms reached the shores, they would surprise the enemies and start killing them by firing at them with their guns.

The stories sounded so dreadful, full of action like in modern day movies and kids would ask him questions such as: "Tah, how does it feel killing the enemy with your gun and seeing him dying in front of you?" He would reply, "war is war, if you pitied the enemy, then the enemy will kill you instead." "Tah, what did the enemy do to become an enemy to you?" He would reply, "the enemy was going to come and kill everybody in my country if I did not kill him." Then we would clap our hands to applaud Tah as our hero. Some children would ask him, "what is a ship?" and Tah would respond that it was a type of large vehicle with rooms, toilets, etc., moving in the seas - a type of water body which had no end! Tah Nujala was so full of humour but many of the village folks did not pay him regular visits. He usually talked to us about countries and continents like Europe, Asia, Japan, India, Vietnam, Germany where they had visited as soldiers before returning to Africa. His hearing had suffered a bit which he attributed to the many gun shots during World War I. After Tah Nujala's tales, we would comment that war was such a very bad thing though most of the male kids said they would become soldiers just like him when they grew up. Many of us suggested that the countries Tah Nujala had visited were fictitious while some thought they were found somewhere in heaven. Sometimes we asked Tah Nujala to speak to us in German and he would utter some words like "Ich bin kranken" and we would all laugh and ask him what it meant and he would say "I am sick". Sometimes, he changed the words and as we walked back to our homes, we would repeat the words he had muttered. When we got home, we would tell our respective parents that we were now capable of speaking German!

Tah Nujala was eventually baptised when he was about eighty years old and was christened, Nicodemus. His godfather was my uncle, Ajuenekoh, who was only about fifteen years then. The older Christian men refused to be his godfather because Nicodemus was allegedly capable of witchcraft. Ajuenekoh and his friends, including the old man's grandson had spent several days looking up for a Christian name in the bible for Nujala. I heard them arguing over two names: Methuselah and Nicodemus. In the end, they agreed on the latter because according to them the name reflected the man's character. They argued that even though Nujala was as old as Methuselah in the bible, nobody knew when he was born, and no one knew what positive impact Methuselah had contributed to human progress.

His wife, Ma Ngwebanchoh was so frightened by the stories of war killings recounted by her husband that she always told Ndih that she would not continue to live with a killer husband like him. She alleged that the blood of the innocent people spilled in the distant lands by her husband had blocked his ears from hearing. She preferred to stay at her farmhouse at Alahbechuong where her son lived, where he often provided her with lots of fish and fresh meat from wild animals – a factor that made her prefer to live in the farmhouse instead of spending time with her husband. She would tell her friends that "if he did not have magical powers, how on earth could he have killed so many people in battle in distant lands and come back home safely and unharmed?" She would say it was difficult for her to live with such a person because he could wake up one night and strangle her, confusing her for an enemy! She said the man spoke in strange languages when he was angry. Were it not for his grandson and his friend, my uncle Ajuenekoh, the poor old ex-soldier who had defended his colonial masters with such bravery, would have died alone at his own home without any financial or moral support from his colonial masters. As I grew up, I eventually learned that all the ex-service men who fought on the side of their German colonial master had suffered the same fate. Not a dime was ever paid to them for their services rendered to Germany in her lost wars.

Ndih would comfort her friend by saying she didn't think her husband was a wicked man or wanted to kill anyone. She blamed the German colonial government for conscripting and sending him on those terrible adventures – about which he had little or no choice. Despite her attempts, Ndih's explanation never convinced the frightened princess. That's why she visited her husband and grandson only on the *mbindos,* the Market days. The fifteen-year-old boy Newhenechu was so courageous and could cook, clean the house and sometimes would bathe his ailing granddad.

During his baptism ceremony, Tah Nujala was asked by the pastor to commit his life to God by throwing away any magical items or unholy stuff in his keeping. The new convert gave away his handbag which contained all his souvenirs from foreign lands to be thrown away. Ajuenekoh, the young godfather, gripped by the fear of the handbag's content, grabbed it and rushed to a nearby river and threw away the bag of souvenirs into the rapid flowing water, much to the relief of his absentee wife Mah Ngwebancho and other terrified villagers. She only returned to her home during the poor man's burial but would frequently seek refuge at night at my grandmother's house because she believed her deceased husband's ghost would haunt her because she neglected him during his final days. Her grandson loved his grandfather very much. He would remind us that his grandmother had the tendency to exaggerate her account of things and that she frequently told white lies. When Tah Nujala died, many kids of my age missed him. The poor veteran had contributed immensely to broaden our tender minds about the geography of the world. He had laid a strong foundation for world history in our young minds. Later in life, I came to understand that uncle Ajuenekoh needed a male role model in his life and Tah Nujala had served this role effectively. This explains why he was so attached to the old man since his own father had passed away when he was much younger. He and his friend Newhenechou wept so bitterly at Tah Nujala's funeral.

Ndih's other friend Mah Mabifor lived much further away, about a kilometre from Ndih's house, in one of the many valleys of Alahtene. Her compound had a small stream running through it and could only be compared to the garden of Eden because it contained a wide variety of tropical delicious fruits. During the holidays, her compound would be full of many grandchildren - because she had eight daughters and a son. All types of birds also perched on trees in her compound including the rare birds whose feathers were used for traditional decorations by the king of Alahbukum. Young boys loved to shoot at the birds on the treetops with their catapult known as "rubber guns". Ripe bananas were always available in abundance and that's where I first saw kids, each of whom nearly finished a big bunch of ripe bananas.

Mah Mabifor was such a jovial and beautiful old lady, always cracking jokes and praising everyone for the least effort made. Her praises usually earned her a lot of gifts as she would call most people with phrases such as "rare species", "something hard to find", "a strong tree with thorns", "rare precious stones", etc. Many people loved the way she praised them and would readily send someone to buy her a bottle of smulgri beer as a gift. However, hardly would the person have left her presence, when she would recount a horrible story of the person's misdeeds and insult the person behind their back. I frequently eavesdropped on her conversations with Ndih during which she would praise people in their presence but backbite them immediately they left. I was often intrigued by this attitude. It turned out that most Alahbukum princesses behaved in similar manner. They hardly pointed out the truth or anyone's faults in their presence and would later add that "this is how commoners are deceived."

On market days, Ndih and her three friends would dress up in their finest *akabas,* sit in their favourite spot – that is, on Ndih's veranda where they had a good view of the market. They would eat some achu after an appetiser of what was popularly called "turning plantains" – that is, green plantains cooked with palm oil, smoked meat, dried fish, bitter leaves and some spices. They would smoke their respective tobacco pipes while recounting old time stories. There was Tah Njikekeh, an elderly man who frequently visited them, trekking from another village to attend the market. He always brought a calabash of sweet raffia palm wine carried on a stick hung on his shoulder with kola nuts in his handbag. His presence always made the old ladies visibly happy. I was particularly fond of the old man because he made Ndih happy. He would also bring me puff-puff which he carefully wrapped and carried in his handbag. Because of the jovial atmosphere his presence always created, I used to look forward to his arrival each market day and would run to meet him on his arrival. I would carry his handbag woven with raffia fibre and rest it near the old ladies. The joy of having him around made me wish the market day would come faster. Eventually, I learnt when the old man passed away that he was indeed Ndih's boyfriend – that is, after my granddad died several years earlier. We attended Tah Njikekeh's funeral and Ndih seemed quite shaken by the man's death. We spent the night after the funeral and his children and brothers who all knew Ndih, took good care of us.

Later, I also learnt that Ndih's three friends were actually her aunts who also happened to be her age mates. Ndih's father was a Prince of Alahbukum and his own father was the king known as "Conqueror of the Earth." He allegedly had one hundred wives because every clan sought to marry off their most beautiful daughters to the king. Sometimes, the notables would go on expeditions throughout the country in search of new wives for the king. Once they spotted a very beautiful girl, they would descend from their horseback and place a cowry bangle on her wrist, and then accompany her to her parents' compound to inform the parents that their daughter had been chosen as a future queen. It was also common for the notables to choose the prettier of a set of female twins. Consequently, many women started coaching their daughters on how to escape the notables' search especially if they heard the sound of horses.

Having a queen in the palace of Alahbukum ensured that notables and headmen from respective villages had easy access to the palace. The king's first wife was highly respected by her co-wives and the entire kingdom. Villagers who had their representatives as queens in the palace usually brought gifts to the most senior wife whose duty it was to train and introduce the new co-wives to the king on specific days according to her whims. Where villagers failed to shower the senior queen with gifts, she would delay the process of introducing their bride to the king.

Ndih's three friends, the senior princesses, recounted an incident during which the king (their father) was strolling through the palace one afternoon and met a very beautiful but forlorn lady sitting in one corner of the palace. He asked her: "pretty lady, who are you?" The young queen who was probably the 96th wife replied in a melancholic voice "I am one of the queens, my name is Queen Yuehnuchem from Alahbukhor." The king then asked further, "for how long have you been in the palace?" and she responded, "for more than two years. My family and village people have not yet brought gifts to the senior queen, so that's why I have not been formally introduced to the king". Then the king asked her, "do you know or have you ever seen the king?" She replied "no, I have never met His Majesty". The king shook his head in disbelief and took her to the inner parts of the palace and introduced himself to the new queen. A few months later, she became pregnant, prompting the other queens to hold a fact-finding meeting. Thereafter, they resolved to banish her from the palace. However, they would first have to inform the king of their decision.

The senior queen went to report about the young queen's pregnancy to the king. "Your Royal Highness" she began, "there is a girl here that was brought from a remote village and I've been training her on royal manners before she could meet with you. She had not even started her probational period when we realised she is pregnant - an abomination in Alahbukum. It therefore means she was not a virgin before her arrival in the palace. For this reason, I have come to request your permission to send her back to her parents." The king listened attentively to the First Lady's story and asked what the girl's name was. "Queen *Yuehnuchem* from Alahbukhor," she said. The king replied "First Lady of Alahbukum, why do you do this type of wicked thing to me? A wife is brought to me from the Alahbukhor clan and you hide her from me just because she is from a poor family, causing her people to hate me. Do you understand the gravity of your act? Do you know that this clan can even wage a war against us because of your act? I met this poor queen and asked her who she was and to my greatest surprise she told me she was one of my wives - a queen. She had been in this palace for more than two years and here you are, telling me she was being trained; how long does your training take? From this day onward, you are no longer in charge of training the new brides! Once a new bride arrives the palace, she must be brought to meet me without delay. I have lost confidence in you. Go back to your section of the palace!" Furious at the First Lady, he turned his back on her and immediately withdrew to his inner courts! News of this incident travelled like wildfire, spread by palace attendants known as *nchindas*. To appease the king, the senior queen's family brought several goats to the palace.

This story explains how younger brides won their liberation to meet the king soon after their arrival at the palace. Henceforth, each queen could give birth to as many children (five to ten children) as she wanted. Prior to this, most queens could only have two kids. My grandmother's "three friends" who were her father's half-sisters each had a sibling because neither their respective mothers' parents nor villages ever brought enough gifts to the First Lady. These three princesses always cursed the First Lady for her greed, wickedness and for imposing such strict orders in the palace. According to them, it seemed the gods had sent her to the king's palace with the sole mandate to reduce the royal population. This explains why in Alahbukum, when the quantity of something to be distributed is small, the question is asked, "as small as this thing is, who should it be given to?" "The nobles or the commoners?" The answer is always that it should be given to the nobles because the commoners are too numerous.

Once when I listened to the old women's stories, I told my grandmother after her friends' departure that the First Lady was very kind. I told her that if I were the senior queen, I would not allow him to marry other women and if he did, I would drive all of them away. Ndih listened to me, shook her head in disbelief and said that in those days, no one could do such a thing for fear of being thrown into the Death Valley by the *kwifor* where you died before reaching the bottom of the valley!

Kwifor was the top-secret masked society of king makers in the kingdom. The king was understood to be a child of kwifor. Long ago, kwifor could sentence criminals, sorcerers, etc., to death. Upon being found guilty, kwifor would send a messenger – *mabuhe* - to execute the sentence. Kwifor had two branches known as *chong* and *takumbeng*. It was believed that only princes, notables and the king could see kwifor and chong. It was also believed in Alahbukum that if a pregnant woman heedlessly watched those two masked *jujus,* she would deliver a baby who looked exactly like them unless she underwent special cleansing rituals. Kwifor and Chong officiated at the funerals of princes, notables and other initiated individuals. Mabuhe the king's messenger and law enforcement wing was the masked institution charged with throwing criminals and other deviants into the Death Valley. The story goes that one day, a certain tough criminal (who had seduced and kidnapped one of the king's wives) and who was facing the death sentence, overpowered Mabuhe and threw the creature into the Death Valley instead and escaped to a distant land. Those who had accompanied Mabuhe waited from a safe distance, but in vain. No one ever saw Mabuhe again and that's how the execution of criminals at the Death Valley ended.

The missing Mabuhe's companions returned to the palace singing a sorrowful song which sent shock waves throughout the kingdom. It was alleged that Mabuhe had been thrown down the steep valley along with the criminal hooked around his neck. However, several years later, news reached Alahbu-kum that the said criminal had survived after throwing Mabuhe into the Death Valley and was spotted alive in a faraway land, happily married with children. Kwifor had planned to send an agent to the distant village to secretly annihilate him but the news leaked before the mission could be carried out.

The execution of criminals at the Death Valley was replaced by banishment to foreign lands. The process was initiated by shooting them with wild garden eggs and blowing wood ash on or after them. Such persons were individuals who had been found guilty of having committed acts classified in Alahbukum as abominable, a list of which was annually communicated in every corner of the kingdom.

Some of Ndih's friends did not like the fact that many children crowded Ndih's home, rendering it a very noisy place. One of them even suggested that Ndih was like a *boma* (baobab) tree where all types of birds, animals, and insects, came to seek refuge, food, and life itself. She also compared the kids to a liana which would attempt to strangle her someday. They said some of those children could be vipers, bees, birds, grasshoppers, witches and other kinds of insects. They cautioned Ndih that some of the children, if left unsupervised, could steal from her. I was shocked by these statements and wondered how a grandmother could say such horrible things about very young children. However, it turned out she was correct because a few of the kids, driven by hunger did steal sugar or honey, spoons and palm oil. Often, the boys would visit the houses of some of the kids and return with a missing spoon. Ndih would ask the delinquent children to refrain from such acts, and often, looking penitent, they would promise to never carry out such acts again.

It was an open secret in Alahtene and throughout the kingdom of Alahbukum that princes and princesses were the king's eyes. This implied that Ndih's three friends were considered spies, informants, whistle-blowers, and gossipers with a tendency to exaggerate matters. They always stayed quiet in most conversations and listened keenly so that they could capture the whole situation (who said or did what). It was known that they kept their father, the king informed on various issues within the kingdom. They usually went back to the palace every week to visit the king and if age prevented them from those frequent trips, (like Ndih's three friends), they would send their sons or daughters to update the king. It was also customary for the king to marry off the princesses to wealthy commoners in the hope that these in-laws could bring some of their wealth to the palace. Since it was known that the princesses gossiped a lot and exaggerated everything they saw or heard, the citizens of Alahtene refrained from discussing sensitive issues in the presence of members of the royal family. If for instance, they heard two families quarrelling in public, they would tell the next person they met that they saw the two persons at daggers drawn on each other's throat. So, the saying went that if a princess saw you going to the toilet multiple times, she would spread the news that you were suffering from cholera. Despite this, the population still respected the princes and princesses by using the honorific "Moo" when addressing them.

8

ACTIVITIES IN NDIH'S HOME

Church Activities

Life at Ndih's house was loaded with activities. There were weekly, seasonal, school, church, non-school days and night activities. Sunday was one of the weekdays I loved best. When I first arrived Ndih's home, I had two pairs of shoes – one, for school and the other for church on Sundays. The first Sunday at Ndih's home, I wore my beautiful pair of black closed toe shoes to church. All the girls of my age group stared at my feet throughout the service and after church, some of them mocked me for wearing shoes. They said Nasi walked "sikosh, sikosh" like a "white man" woman. When I walked, my shoes produced a sound which to their ears sounded like "sikosh, sikosh". I felt so embarrassed and sad, and when I got back home, I told grandma of my resolve not to wear shoes to church on Sunday. She did not object to my proposal. She suggested that if the shoes hurt my feet, then I should no longer wear them. Henceforth, I went about barefooted to fit in with my age mates. Some of them even played football barefooted. Later in life, I would learn that "in the kingdom of the blind, the one-eyed is king" but this didn't apply to my case.

Participating in church activities built very strong values in most kids of my age on such issues as love, truth, honesty, sharing and hard work. Each time church activities were over, Ndih would ask me what we learned from the Sunday school, and I would recount the teacher's lesson for that day. Sometimes, Ndih would correct me if I narrated some aspect of the lesson incorrectly. I would ask her how she knew the different chapters of the bible and she would remind me of the fact that the first church in Alahtene was started by her late husband and that he used to read the bible aloud to her in one of the local languages. She also reminded me that she once held the position of a deacon in that church.

My favourite bible episodes were the exodus of the Israelis from slavery in Egypt to the Promised Land; the miracle of crossing the Red Sea; the healing of the ten lepers by Jesus and only one of them returned to express his gratitude; the parable of the prodigal son which Jesus recounted to his disciples about the son who requested his own inheritance from his father, squandered it and when things went bad for him, he remembered his father and returned to ask him to employ him as just one of his servants. I grew up wondering about the scriptures which guided me on what to expect from humans. My grandma used to remind me that if Jesus healed the ten lepers but only one (who was a foreigner) returned to say thank you, then we as humans should not expect "thanks" from anyone to whom we have rendered a good service. "We must continue to do good anyway", she would say.

Despite the relative peaceful co-existence between the two main churches in Alahtene in those days, an incident led to a dramatic setback in the relationship between Christians of those two churches. Both catechists from the respective denominations were drinking together in one of the pubs at the village market. One of them took out kola nuts from his pocket and broke it as was tradition, then shared it with everyone who was with them. After consuming the kola nuts, drinks, soya and other foodstuffs, the other catechist returned home and could no longer speak. He became paralyzed and news went round that he had been poisoned by the other catechist. He was taken for local treatment where he later died. A resolution was consequently taken by members of the church whose pastor had been accused to no longer admit pupils in the lone primary school of Alahtene which belonged to them. Consequently, children from the bereaved denomination whose catechist had probably died from a stroke were forced to travel for about five miles every morning and evening to attend another school in a distant village. The pupils each carried their books inside boxes made of corrugated iron sheets. They endured this every day, in sunshine or rain for the duration of the school term.

Schooling

The admission process into Infants One (grade one) in the lone school at Alahtene was full of fun and anxiety. It was carried out in front of the whole school assembly in an open field. Parents would bring their young kids for assessment and eventually admission. The head teacher would ask a kid seeking admission to place his or her right hand over his/her head to touch their left ear. Should a child fail to fulfil this, he/she would be sent home with their parents, prompting the older pupils in senior classes to exclaim with pity - "weh". On the other hand, should a kid succeed in touching their left ear, then all the older pupils would shout for joy - "yay". Their exclamations always made the new kids nervous. When I arrived for admission, I was lucky enough to pass that preliminary test by placing my right hand over my head to touch my left ear, which according to local knowledge, suggested that I was at least, six years.

Although tall children had it easy during admissions, this was not always the case for short kids. I remember vividly how one of my age mates who was shorter than me and could not touch her left ear following the stipulated method had to come up with a smart idea to gain admission. Immediately she failed the "ear test", she started singing a popular tune - "school is a good thing, learning is a good thing, I come to school to learn ABC and 1, 2, 3, …" The headmaster was so thrilled that he broke the rule and admitted her immediately based on his observation that her ability to sing a song that was taught to pupils in Infants one, meant that she was ready and indeed loved school. She was later nicknamed by the pupils in senior classes as "school is a good thing". This admission procedure was done as such because back in 1961, most people did not have birth certificates that could readily tell their age. It is fair to guess that the children who attended Infants One ranged in age from six to about ten.

On my first day at school, I wore a new pair of shoes. My classmates frequently looked at my feet and laughed at me. I felt odd to be the only other person in my class with shoes, besides the teacher. The next day, I abandoned the pair of shoes in my desperate attempt to fit in. My teacher who had noticed my shoes the previous day, expressed shock and sought to know what had happened to them. I was embarrassed to tell him I didn't want to be the only child in class with shoes. Without my shoes, walking barefooted became a huge challenge as I had to become accustomed to the pebbles, the sweltering hot sand and dust which roasted the soles of my feet. I soon developed severe blisters on my soles. I also hated it when I hit my toes against stones during the early cold morning on my way to school. This was part of the price I had to pay to fit in with my peers in the village.

School was full of many lively activities - roll call, hygiene inspection, learning, singing, sports, gardening and compound care. Morning hygiene inspection was dreaded by all new pupils. The hygiene teacher frequently carried out a thorough inspection to see whether pupils' hair was unkempt, if they had lice, whether their nails were properly trimmed, if they had brushed their teeth or had a foul mouth odour, if their uniforms were well washed or not and most importantly, if pupils had scabies on their buttocks or jiggers on their toes. Jiggers were believed to originate from fleas that lived with pigs especially in dusty areas. The jiggers would enter people's toes where they would grow big, lay a lot of eggs, and consequently deform the person's toes by making it difficult for him/her to walk properly. It was common in Alahtene to find most young boys with jiggers, a matter that was considered a major health threat in the community.

It was believed that if anyone went through the morning inspection successfully, then it would be a good day for them. The morning inspection also included checking on latecomers, who were always assigned to a separate queue, distinct from the rest of the pupils. It was common for the headmaster to whip the latecomers with his cane; boys on their buttocks and girls on their palms. Some boys who were notorious latecomers would place papers or pieces of carton inside their shorts around their buttocks to dampen the effect of the whips. Some of us feared the headmaster's cane and made every effort to always be on time. Most princes and princesses in Alahbukum dreaded the thought of going to school and be whipped by the headmaster. Their mothers also encouraged them to stay at home because it was considered ill-placed for anyone who was not of royal descent to whip them. Consequently, many of the princes or princesses ended up illiterate.

I loved every aspect of the school curricula, especially the music classes. My class was divided into three rows: the smartest kids sat on the right side of Mr. Barth's desk, the smarter ones in the middle and the smart ones on the left side. I normally sat on the front row on the right side of the teacher's desk. The first day of school was so thrilling and started with introductions. Each pupil had to state his/her name, parents' names and the name of their neighbourhood in the village. One of the oldest pupils did not know his father's name and kept repeating "my father's name is Tahgha" which virtually meant his father's name is "my father". This provoked an uproar of laughter among the pupils and the mate was readily nicknamed "Tahgha". It was customary in Alahtene for children to call their fathers "Tahgha". So, many children ended up not knowing their fathers' real names.

Lunch breaks at school were memorable periods. Most kids hardly brought lunch to school and during breaks, they would juggle from one kid to the next asking to share their food. Most of those who brought something for lunch brought the local staple - achu. Some of the "beggar" kids would ask to take two portions and if the owner accepted, they would cut off a very large portion for themselves and then move on to the next kid. Some kids who never brought lunch ended up begging and eating more food than those who effectively brought their lunch.

Pupils in the early days of Infants One were provided slates and chalk to write letters and figures on. Those who could not use the slates were required to write on the sand which was spread out in front of the classroom. Many pupils went back home from school with white chalk all over their faces and on their school uniform whose regular colour was ash gray. One of my mates who had difficulty with writing, hardly completed his homework. Once when he was asked by the teacher why he had not completed his homework, he responded that the sun had shone so hard on his slate and had wiped out everything he had written. This astonished the entire class and the teacher exclaimed as well, repeating the absurd claims.

During question-and-answer sessions, the kids would thrust their hands into the air saying - "I Sir, I Sir" in rhythm. Occasionally, a kid in Group 3 would be selected by the teacher to give an answer; instead of providing the answer, he would stare into the classroom's ceiling, shake his head saying "mmm, I have forgotten the answer!" This would stir a lot of laughter among the pupils including Mr. Barth.

During music classes, most pupils on the left row would struggle with the lyrics. This meant that they usually murmured rather than sing the words. If the teacher yelled at them, they would be so shaken and even forget the melody. At the end of the music class, marks would be assigned to the respective groups and the smartest group always came on top while the others struggled. On one occasion, the teacher asked me to join the third row to boost their morale in singing "King Makers" of Alahbukum. I was so saddened by the fact that the pupils in this group struggled with their singing, so I sang as loud as I could, but the group still emerged last when grades were assigned. I burst out in tears and the teacher, seeking to console me, requested the whole class to clap for me. This worked the magic as I smiled happily with a sense of satisfaction.

Textbooks were provided in school and at the end of the school day, pupils were required to leave them in their lockers underneath the benches. I loved reading especially because most of the textbooks had beautiful and colourful pictures in them. Homework had to be done at night, but I usually did mine immediately I got home in order to make use of daylight and save the kerosene needed to light Ndih's bush lamp. Kerosene was very expensive by village standards. When we ran out of fuel for the lamp, we would use a piece of broken calabash with a bit of palm oil placed in it. This helped to light up the room so we could complete our homework. When we finished our homework, we would put out the light and begin storytelling, our faces lit by the glow of fire from Ndih's fireplace. This was my favourite moment because I learned a lot of stories from the boys and girls who were our neighbours. My favourite stories were those that recounted the exploits of tortoise who was considered the most cunning animal amongst my people. The stories were always accompanied by songs, which I quickly learned and would use them to scare away grain-eating birds and animals from Ndih's farms.

Sport was another exciting school activity, especially because it entailed winning and losing. The games we played included football, handball, basketball, track and field of various distances, high jump, long jump, running while wearing long jute bags called *mukuta*, running and picking eggs with spoons for girls, among others. I loved sports especially track and field. It was thanks to our experience in track and field that my uncle, Ajuenekoh and I pursued a yellow female nursing monkey and just when we were about to catch up with it, it sprang even faster, letting its baby to fall off its breast. We captured the baby monkey, took it home and named it Adamu. We raised Adamu and guarded it jealously. Adamu was the best pet I ever had. He ate every food we ate but did not like dogs. If you heard Adamu cry, then it was a sign that a dog was approaching. I made sure that dogs did not come near Adamu except Lucky, our hunting dog. Adamu accompanied me everywhere except school or church. He would stay home with Ndih or perched on a nearby fruit tree to wait for our return.

Adamu was such an intelligent animal and knew exactly when one was happy or sad. If we all went away from home, Adamu would climb trees near the house and stay there to wait for our return. If Adamu was confronted by a dog, it would run quickly to me, climb on my shoulder, and once comforted by the safety of my presence, I would pick up a stick to chase away the dog. Adamu was about two years old when I came back home one day and couldn't find it. My friends and I searched for it in all our neighbours' homes to no avail. We were devastated to have lost him. The thought that Adamu may have been caught, killed, cooked and eaten in pepper soup made me even more devastated. Ndih comforted me by suggesting that we ought to think positively about its fate; she suggested that perhaps, Adamu would have a better life if it had been stolen and sold to tourists from the big city. Until this day, I suspected that one of the older boys, Ajuenekoh's friend might have stolen Adamu, but I couldn't figure out what he may have done with the poor innocent and loving animal. With Adamu's disappearance, I lost a true friend and favourite pet. My love for nature and conservation was kindled by Adamu's story as I pondered about the trauma its mother must have gone through after we snatched it from her.

Manual work in school was another activity I enjoyed. This involved clearing the school field, cultivating and tending crops at the school farm, flower and tree planting. The older pupils were tasked with clearing the school field and other parts using their machetes while the younger ones raked the grass and dumped it at a designated spot for compost. We had so much fun raking the grass and transporting it to the compost area because we devised techniques to complete our task in the shortest time possible. We would place two long sticks together close to each other and pile the grass on it. Then two pupils would carry the load and walk as quickly as they could to dump their load and come back for more.

I also enjoyed spending time at the school farm. It was divided into three plots. During farming season, the corn section would be full of tall stalks of corn because of the manure from the compost. The yam plot had dozens of sticks next to the yam stems to guide the climbers. The headmaster frequently ordered the big boys to bring animal dung from their respective homes for the yam plot. The last plot grew cassava which always seemed to flourish with huge stems. It was known that some villagers would clandestinely harvest the cassava leaves during the dry season to cook them as vegetables.

The school garden was the most beautiful part of the school. It had a variety of flowers. Students were often required to bring flowers for planting in the school garden. We also went out after school to the savannah in search of flowering plants or any beautiful plant we could find. The nature study teacher would receive all these plants and plant them in the school garden plot. She wrote the botanical names of each plant next to it and would ensure that plants were grouped by family. During the dry season, we would water the garden in the mornings and loved to see it blooming. In our nature study classes, we would study the botanical names of the flowers and some of the flowerless plants. During exams, we would be quizzed on their names, their uses, colours, etc. Flowers from the garden were usually presented to visiting dignitaries, to decorate the headteacher's office and the church, especially at important Christian feasts like Corpus Christi, Easter, etc. Some of the flowers were also planted all over the school campus.

Handwork was another thrilling activity because we made items such as bamboo baskets, bamboo stools, woven bags, caps, woven trays from grass, wall mats from raffia leaves, among others. We also learnt the art of knitting and crocheting during handwork sessions. My favourite activity was weaving baskets and sewing aprons. After I had mastered how to stitch with the needle, I would ask my grandmother for her torn dresses to stitch.

How we Sang the Wrong Song at an Important School Event

A team of government officials were scheduled to visit the village to assess the needs of the community. My primary school was chosen as the venue that will host the guests and community members. Although we had just a few days to the event, our class teacher hurriedly taught us a welcome song. Of the forty pupils in the class, I was chosen to conduct the choir because I had mastered the lyrics. On the set day, we were invited to deliver our welcome song to the assembly of villagers, notables, chiefs, the school staff, senior pupils and most importantly, our august visitors. Unfortunately, I succumbed to an attack of stage fright and forgot the lyrics which we had hurriedly practised for about three days. I tried hard to tune the song but could not find the right words. I then asked one of my classmates to remind me of the song's lyrics, but she too had forgotten. To save face, I tuned another song unknown to most of the pupils and we struggled along, much to the amusement of the crowd while our class teacher looked on, bewildered. Despite the unfolding disaster, I conducted the song with much confidence.

The visitors thought we were singing in our local language while the villagers were delighted that their kids had mastered a song in the English language. After our embarrassing performance, we left the podium completely frustrated. I also felt sick with disappointment for letting my class and teacher down. However, the next day, our teacher praised us for our courage and the fact that we had improvised a new song for the visitors. Although this comforted us a bit, my grandmother's advice after this event has stayed on with me since then. She cautioned that each time I had to carry out a public performance, perhaps, a speech or song, I should not worry about the crowd but look instead above people's heads, not their faces.

The School Head Teacher

The school headmaster taught the senior classes all subjects: English language, Arithmetic, History, Geography, Nature's Study and Civics. He lived very far from the school premises but came very early to school every morning on his bicycle. He knew the names of almost all the over four hundred pupils in his school. He always moved about in school with his cane in hand. It was said that in his office, there was a bible proverb written on the wall: "spare the rod and spoil the child". He applied this proverb to the letter by whipping any pupil who broke the rules. If he caught a pupil walking idly in the school premises during classes, he would flog him or her and send the delinquent pupil racing back to class. He was in charge of proclaiming the results of every class in the general assembly room at the end of every school term. Some of the produce from the school farm were normally taken to the head teacher's home and a portion of it was distributed among the teachers and the rest sold to the villagers.

The head teacher was a very honest man and was highly respected by the entire village and his staff but dreaded by the pupils. Some pupils even forgot their own names in fright when they had an encounter with him. In addition to being the general supervisor and disciplinarian, the head teacher also read the final promotion examination results for the whole school from Infants One to Standard Six (eight classes). I remember one occasion when I came out first in my class (standard Four) and the final results were read by the head teacher. Prior to the proclamation of the school results, I had been playing with my classmates during which my uniform got torn near my chest. So, in the general assembly hall where the entire school was assembled awaiting the results, I hid myself at the back in an attempt from being noticed. Unfortunately, it was customary for the names of the top three pupils in each class to be called and for them to come to the podium to be cheered. The headmaster started: "the first person in this class is a girl and her name is Nasi." I was startled and shy because of my torn uniform. My heart throbbed inside me. Then the older boys and girls in the senior classes started pushing me to go to the podium but I resisted. So, they lifted me up and took me to the podium. Mr. Michros, the head teacher looked at me closely and said, "despite her torn uniform, she has braved it to be the first in a class of over forty pupils". I immediately burst into tears and was only calmed by the cheering and amicable screams of the older pupils who after the name of the third best pupil had been called, came up again and lifted me back to my hiding spot at the back of the hall.

Despite my outstanding performance, I also feared coming face to face with the head teacher except on occasions when the final results were read and I was confident to emerge top.

Later in life, I learnt that the head teacher's real name was Mr. Nicholas Abassa but the villagers called it Michros because they could not pronounce Nicholas properly. He is fondly remembered for the renovations he made to the school's two buildings which remain visible to this day.

Alahtene's Pioneer Secondary School Girl

*M*iss was the local word used by the villagers to address the first girl from Alahtene who went to secondary school. She might have been in the third or fourth year in secondary school when I came to live with Ndih Maghrebong. On one occasion, we met her on the road during the holidays and my friends and I were so excited to greet and get acquainted with her. She was so soft spoken, neat, always wore a smile and appeared respectful. She was the one who inspired most of the kids of Alahtene to consider going to secondary school. It turned out that she was the first daughter of the head of the village council of elders, (*Tanikruh Akohchiri*). She had so many brothers and sisters although her siblings gained fame simply for being identified as siblings to "Miss". Whenever we met Miss, my friends and I would return home chattering happily and imagining the day we would see the four walls of a secondary school. None of us had ever seen a secondary school, let alone one for girls. We were told that the lone girls-only secondary school in the country was in a faraway big city and it would take a day's journey in the cargo lorries to get there. The school was called Queen's College and it was rumoured that students who attended it were expected to master the manners of the Queen of England because they were destined for high society - the successful few elites. Although we were inspired by Miss's manners, some of the boys thought she was too proud because she was reserved and talked very little.

Most of Miss's siblings did not attend primary school because her secondary school tuition had allegedly drained all her father's resources. It was rumoured that her father expected her to complete secondary school, get a job and then sponsor her siblings through primary school. Miss's father had five wives and some of them told Ndih they would not allow their own children to become *dooms* - the term used to describe illiterates in Alahtene - like themselves. Eventually, some of them succeeded to enrol their children at the lone village primary school that required a tuition of about US$2 in today's currency. Although this amount may appear small, it took ages for them to raise this kind of money.

Immediately Miss graduated from secondary school, an elite from another village wooed and married her. This brought an end to the hopes of her siblings who had expected that she would sponsor them through elementary school. Thus it was, that those whose mothers had not taken the initiative to enrol them ended up as palm or raffia wine tappers to this day.

9

DOMESTIC CHORES

Farming and animal breeding

At Ndih's house, every season was devoted to the cultivation of specific types of food crops. Except for rice, we harvested most of our food from Ndih's farms. Some of her farms were cultivated by younger women who considered Ndih as their mother. Some who had borrowed Ndih's money and were unable to repay asked to work on her farm too. When these ladies came to cultivate, they would spend the entire day. We would cook food and buy raffia palm wine from our neighbour for the women. During such occasions, the woman who had the honour of breaking the first soil with her hoe was usually the person recognised by her peers as the most hardworking. As they tilled the soil, they would sing creative and joyful songs to keep their spirits high.

Inspired by these women, my five friends and I would do "nseige" – a type of rotational work scheme which entailed taking turns to work in each person's plot until everyone had benefited. The beneficiaries were normally my friends' mothers, and in my case, my grandmother. We would do about three rotations each farming season during which we cultivated the fields and planted various types of food crops. Although locals did not use fertilizers, pesticides or modified seeds, most farms often had very high yields.

Ndih also had two pigs (male and female), three goats and several chickens. The breed of chickens would lay several eggs and when they hatched, the chicks and mother hen would eat most of the vegetables around the homestead. They would also dig up seeds from the farm and enter the house to look for food. It was easier to handle the pigs and goats than the chickens. We also had to keep an eye on the hawks because they would attempt to carry away the chicks. Hence, we spent hours watching the skies and when we saw them, we would shout "wah, wah, wah" to scare them off. Sometimes, when a hawk was about to capture one of the chicks, the mother hen would fly towards the predator in a bid to scare it off. Once, we witnessed one of the hens attack and kill a hawk that had almost captured its chick. We picked up the hawk, boiled some water and plugged its feathers thereafter. We then stewed the meat in our well-spiced soup. I used to marvel at the bravery of the hens in protecting their chicks. Ndih would remind me that the role of mothers was to provide food and protection from danger to their children as mother hen did for her chicks. As for the hawks, many people from Alahtene believed that they were witches and wizards transformed into birds from a neighbouring kingdom. Locals believed that the witches visited Alahtene during the day to steal their chickens because residents of Alahtene allegedly raised the best indigenous chickens. According to the story we heard, locals claimed that some Alahtene hunters followed one of the hawks and discovered its

landing spot in the neighbouring kingdom. Watching stealth-
ily, they saw the bird drop the chicken and then transformed
itself into a human. The hunters also noticed that this person's
compound was full of chickens which he may have stolen from
surrounding kingdoms. Furthermore, the legend holds that
one day, some of the hawks arrived Alahtene and two of them
got caught by two local hens. The hawks were then tethered
and placed at a corner of the homestead but within two hours
or less, some residents of the neighbouring kingdom arrived
Alahtene and requested that the birds be sold to them. The
chickens' owner overpriced the two hawks which they paid
because as it were, they were supposedly seeking to liberate
the witches from captivity.

Ndih also knew so much about plants and their uses.
Despite her poor eyesight, she would show me different types
of herbs and taught me about the corresponding diseases each
could treat. She would uproot a specific herb and tell me, "this
is what you have to uproot (several stems or cut its leaves) and
squeeze into the water contained in a calabash placed under a
plantain stem for fowls." Once they drank from it, they won't
be sick. She also had different herbal regimens for pigs and
goats. To treat the goats, she would place some salt in a wooden
mortar along with certain herbs. Upon consuming the salt
and the herbs, the goats would be relieved from diarrhoea,
sneezing or coughing. I could tell they were always excited
to see me open the door to their barn because they expected
me to have brought them salt. Ndih was such an astute herder
so much so that most animal epidemics that befell Alahtene
hardly affected her poultry, goats or pigs. She knew when to
begin preventive action when there was an impending livestock
disease. She would ask me to drive away neighbours' animals

that had strayed into our compound. When I became older, I learnt that these actions were the most effective method to prevent the spread of livestock diseases.

Ndih's many farms frequently needed weeding, mulching and most importantly, driving off the birds and animals that sought to destroy the crops. We placed scarecrows at various angles of the farms which we had made from old red or black clothes. The afternoons were the ideal time for me to visit the farm to scare away the animals by singing. The usual suspects were birds, squirrels, giant and cane rats as well as stray goats. After singing alone, I would hold imaginary conversations with the animals, most often insulting them as such: "you all have four legs and hands, yet you prefer to steal rather than to work; do not dare come near this farm or I will deal with you." I would move from one corner of the farm to the other, singing, shouting and sometimes imitating a hawk. Somehow, I thought the animals and birds always imagined that I was not alone. Whenever my uncle was playing checkers or any of his favourite games, I would be accompanied by our loyal hunting dog, Lucky.

During harvest season, we harvested plenty of corn, groundnuts, potatoes, various types of beans, sweet potatoes, a variety of vegetables, coco-yams, various species of yams, Colocasia, plantains and bananas. Many of the food stuff could last until the following year. Crops such as cassava, pumpkins, and macabo were in abundance in Ndih's numerous farm plots. Ndih taught us many simple conservation methods for the harvested crops. Corn, groundnuts, and beans were stored in the barn (on the inner roof of the house where the smoke from the house dried them). Cocoyams and yams were stored by digging up a small trench near the house; we would place dry plantain leaves inside, then place the yams or cocoyams inside, cover them with more dry leaves and then finally, pour cold wood ash over them. This technique kept the produce from rotting or attack by insects or viruses. Pumpkins were conserved by placing them on shelves outside the house, away from direct sun rays. Cassava was preserved by soaking them in a big clay pot which fermented and was eventually transformed into cassava fufu. This process eliminated the bitterness from white cassava. The red cassava on the other hand was not bitter, so we would pound them into a type of fufu called "akwaah" which could be eaten with okra, dry fish and egusi (melon seed) soup.

Egusi was preferred as a soup thickener and obtained from a variety of pumpkin. The melon plant was usually planted with accompanying sticks to support it because it was a well-known climber. Sometimes we would be overwhelmed with too much farm work, and when this happened, we would leave the melon stems to creep around the garden which ended up bearing a lot of melons. When we harvested the melons, we would dig a large hole and dump them inside to ferment. After three or four days, we would dig out the melons, collect their seeds, wash and eventually dry them in the sun. We would then crack the shells and use the seeds to prepare a variety of dishes such as egusi pudding, and vegetable dishes, etc.

The barn was one of the most interesting spots in the house. When my friends and I played hide-and-seek around the house, I would use the ladder to climb into the barn (which was part of the ceiling) to hide after which I would pull the ladder after me. It was usually difficult for friends to guess that I had hid myself in the barn.

Corn, groundnuts and beans were usually kept in the barn.

A ladder was used to climb into the barn where the corn, groundnuts and beans were deposited on the barn's floor, each according to its own specific spot. We would spread the fresh produce carefully and every three to four days, uncle Ajuenekoh or I would climb into the barn to rotate them to ensure they were getting dry. Corn was placed around the spot directly on top of the fire hearth, followed by fresh groundnuts and then beans. When the items were dried to our satisfaction, we would put them in big bags and shell them by hitting the bags with sticks. As for groundnuts, we would remove them once dried and place them in special baskets, cover them with dry plantain leaves and return them to the barn until the next farming season. We would also shell some and roast them. These were then used for preparing soup.

Sometimes, when Ndih was away, Ajuenekoh and his friends would use long solid sticks to wiggle some room between the bamboos in the barn. When they succeeded, some of the groundnuts would fall on the floor and they'll pick and eat them. Although I often caught them pulling off these tricks, I never reported them to Ndih because I was concerned that they would bully me in her absence. This was especially so because they had nicknamed me "Report Card" for always telling Ndih everything that had happened during her absence. I would be watching the road and immediately I saw her coming, I would run to meet her, collect her handbag, search for its contents, grab anything edible from it and then begin to report my uncle's misdeeds. I would end by cautioning her not to ask because Ajuenekoh would pinch my ears in her absence. However, Ndih always figured out what had gone wrong. For example, upon seeing black sooth on the floor, she would ask Ajuenekoh why he had climbed into the ceiling. Ajuenekoh would look at me sternly and then stick out his tongue at me. This was his way of telling me that I'd be in trouble when grandma goes out for a visit. Consequently, I always did my best to avoid being left alone with uncle Ajuenekoh.

Fetching Firewood and water

Each time we went to our farms, we would fetch firewood for cooking, heating the house on cold nights and for drying our farm produce. This meant that we needed a constant supply of firewood all year round. If for some reason, we ran out of wood, she would remove a few bamboos from the floor of her bed to use as fuelwood. So, it was my duty to fetch as much firewood from every tree, (mostly dry fallen branches), dead stumps and even small trees that had been felled and left to dry. Raffia palm stumps also served as a regular source of firewood. Her stash of firewood was stored outside around the house foundation.

Another important chore was to fetch water for cooking and for many other purposes. The stream from where we fetched water for cooking was about a kilometre away. We also collected spring water for drinking from a small forest about a kilometre away but in a different direction from the stream. The main containers we used for carrying water were calabashes. Sometimes, a calabash would fall off from one's head and break into pieces with its contents spilling on the ground. When this happened, I'd return home crying all the way from the stream and Ndih would comfort me by saying I should be more careful next time. Sometimes, she would say that she hoped I had not been singing and dancing without paying much attention to the calabash on my head. Well, that's exactly what had happened each time I crashed my calabash.

Cooking

At my grandmother's, we made sure the fireside was always aglow. This was done by placing a huge quantity of wood ash on the logs. Thus, they would burn gently throughout the night or day as needed. Sometimes, if the logs didn't conserve enough fire, we would have to light the fireside once again. If my efforts didn't succeed, I would either kick the logs apart or pour water on them and then burst into tears.

If the logs happened to burn out, one mechanism to revive them would be to hit a special pair of stones against each other – in between which we had some cotton balls obtained from palm nuts. Ndih was so skilful in hitting the pair of stones with the *nkukure* as the cotton was called. Soon, there would be smoke followed by fire. Ndih would encourage me to learn how to hit the stones, but my efforts always ended in vain. Sometimes, we would be unable to use our special stones if they were wet (especially if we had taken them to the farm to make fire for roasting food), then we would borrow fire from a neighbour's hearth. It required special skills to fetch and handle the fire from a neighbour's house. To accomplish this, we would use several pieces of split wood tied together, then we'd place the wood in the neighbour's fire and once they caught fire, we'd swiftly but gently, carry the fire back to our own home. This process was always a huge challenge for any newcomer.

The cooking pots were made of baked clay – their reddish colour, the result of skilled baking. One of the biggest clay pots in Ndih's house was used to preserve drinking water which always stayed cool. Eventually, when I became accustomed to homes with a refrigerator, I always remembered how similar Ndih's waterpot had served as a natural fridge.

Cooking was by custom, a female activity. Ndih was

meticulous in instructing me about how to cook every meal she prepared. We would spend memorable times together during which I would ask questions about every ingredient and how to use them in preparing various dishes. Ndih had a small storage box or pantry that hung above her fireside – known as *tetareh* which contained various dried or smoked condiments - mushrooms, fish, smoked meat, spices, tadpoles, pepper, garden eggs among others. Ndih would use at least a combination of these items for every meal she prepared.

It was almost certain that each time we prepared certain meals like rice and stew or achu, we would have some "unwanted" visitors - Ajuenekoh's friends or age mates. Either the aroma from the stew or the sound of pounding normally alerted them. Grandmother would caution me to use my intellect and not my strength in pounding the achu. These uninvited guests usually spent most of their time playing checkers, hunting or fishing. They would sell most of their catch and then show up at Ndih's house for supper. Ndih would admonish them in pidgin English: "work, no, chop, yes!", to which they would burst out laughing and respond that Ndih's English was too "grammatical" for them to understand.

Besides Ajuenekoh's friends, it was common to have many neighbourhood kids around Ndih's fireside, waiting for food. It seemed to me that these children were always hungry. While some of them helped to keep the fire going, others would pinch or pull each other's jaws or try to start a fight. Ndih had a peculiar way of detecting their hunger. Sometimes Ndih would ask them to stop yelling at each other and then ask if they were angry? The younger ones who were generally less shy would respond "yes Ndih" in chorus, while the bigger kids would say the junior ones had insulted them the previous days. The kids who wanted the meal being cooked to be ready sooner would go outside and bring more wood for Ndih's fireside. However, once everyone had eaten to their fill, even those who had previously stated that they were angry with such and such a person would show no sign of anger. Everybody would resume playing with each other. Ndih would tell me that each time I saw a group of children fighting or expressing anger towards each other, I should know that they were hungry. This has always reminded me of the proverb that a hungry man is an angry man.

Dangerous lessons in Bravery

Most often when Ndih was away from home, Ajuenekoh and his friends would organise "wrestling competitions" amongst kids: girls against boys of our age group. They would initiate the process by claiming that the younger boys had told them earlier that if given the opportunity, they could thrash all the girls of their age group. They would follow up their claim by placing five boys in a row opposite five girls. Next, they would draw a line on the sandy ground with a stick, after which they would collect or pick something like a strand of hair from one of the girls and take to the boys. Then, they would say to the younger boys: "if you did really say you can beat these girls, then blow on this strand of hair." One of the most courageous boys would blow off the hair and the fight would start by all the boys crossing the line on the ground and pinching the jaws of their opponents. Thus it was that the group fight would start and any kid who wrestled her opponent to the ground and sat on top of him or her was declared winner. Frequently, a girl would wrestle one of the boys to the ground and sit on top of him much to the delight of Ajuenekoh and his mischievous friends.

It was also common for some of the younger boys of our age group, after having suffered defeat, would cry out and call for another round on the grounds that they were not well prepared for the first round. However, Ajuenekoh and his friends would declare that the session was over. They would encourage the defeated boys to practise their skills among themselves and to prepare for a next session when the opportunity would come up. Ndih had no knowledge of these secret fights because Ajuenekoh and his friends warned all participants not to tell their parents. When I grew up, I wondered why anyone would take such interest in seeing young children wrestle each other but I guess for Ajuenekoh and his friends, it was like watching a modern live wrestling match.

10

HARVESTS FROM THE WILD

There were several cherished plants, fruits and fungi in the forest and open fields depending on the season. Uncle Ajeunekoh and I frequently went into the forest to harvest wild fruits such as "bush cocoa", sweet and sour fruits called *achohe*, and nuts from raffia palms amongst others. The wild cocoa fruit was sweet, and juicy. It felt slippery in the mouth and easily slid into one's stomach. Each time we ate it, Ajuenokoh would ask me where I had kept the seed and the first time I told him that I had swallowed it, he pretended to be sympathetic and told me that the seed was not meant to be swallowed. He added that the seed would germinate in my stomach, then grow through my head and people would come to harvest the fruit off my head. Believing what he had said as fact, I started crying. Ndih told me not to worry because seeds can't grow in people's stomachs and that the intestines don't contain soil. She added that when next my uncle scared me with such outrageous claims, I should ask him to show me someone with a wild cocoa on his/her head. While this consoled me, Ajuenekoh often laughed at my initial naivety.

Mushrooms (bohe)

Residents of Alahtene consumed a lot of wild mushrooms, but nobody ever thought mushrooms could be farmed. During the rainy season, our team went out to harvest mushrooms in the wild. We usually started very early in the morning, each person carrying a big basket (woven with bamboo thread) and a cutlass with which to dig up the fungi. We would get back home about mid-day extremely hungry (although we would have snacked on guavas, mangoes and sweet wild berries). There were mainly six types of mushrooms: white mushrooms, yellow mushrooms, very small sized mushrooms, middle sized, brown mushrooms that grew on dead tree trunks, and very large ones. Ndih had taught me how to identify nontoxic mushrooms from their nice scent. She told me that should you harvest and eat a toxic mushroom, it could provoke madness or death. While in the fields, we would do everything to avoid the mushrooms that had an unpleasant scent. When we were done gathering the mushrooms, we would take them home, smoke and break them into pieces, then store them in well-corked calabashes. We would then use them throughout the year to prepare various types of soups especially achu soup, add them to a variety of porridge dishes like plantains, cocoyams, potatoes, beans. They were so delicious and tasted like smoked beef!

Green Grasshoppers (*Mengueneh*)

A type of green grasshoppers usually came to Alahtene at the beginning of the rainy season when the grass was all green. The insects usually flew into the grassfields from some distant land and made a special noise which enabled the older folks in the village to easily locate them. For a newcomer like me, it was difficult to distinguish the green grasshoppers from the grass, but gradually, I learnt how to detect them as well. Once I became acquainted with their behaviours, I noticed that they usually buried their heads within the green grass with their legs lifted upwards. This made it difficult for them to be easily recognized but equally difficult for them to escape from being collected. Green grasshopper harvesting was done very early in the morning before sunrise. On such days, we would be awoken by early risers before six o'clock, with the following sounds: *uh huh, uh huh*! We would jump out of bed, grab any available jute bags, large calabashes or rubber bucket with covers and run off in the direction of the crier. It took us a short while to get to the hills because we preferred to run to dampen the effect of the chilly morning atmosphere. Grasshoppers were considered a delicacy in Alahtene, so we were expected to gather as much as possible, some of which we would share with our uncles, aunts and grandparents in order to receive a blessing from them. So, we worked extremely hard, determined to collect the most we could afford before the sun rose – after which they usually flew away. With a bag or bucket full, we would head home chatting happily as we looked forward to breakfast.

Sometimes, if the hills were not foggy, we would climb to the top after the harvest to admire the distant lands. There, we imagined how as grown-ups, we would visit those distant lands which we imagined must be full of attractions. Little did we know then that our imaginations had unconsciously created in us, the desire to travel and explore the world.

Grass Beetles (*Merisingne*)

O ther edible insects we harvested from the fields were a variety of beetles of different colours. These insects appeared or migrated to Alahtene during the dry season and made the savannah grass their main habitat. They usually hung on the tall grass tops where they ate the seeds of the elephant grass. Many birds and green grass snakes fed on the beetles. We would harvest the beetles and put them inside calabashes and carry them home after which we plugged their wings and legs, washed them, then prepared them in a stew of tree tomatoes and pepper. They were also delicious to eat with boiled cocoyams, plantains or cassava. Some people also spiced their egusi puddings with the insects. These beetles had three main colours – gold, green and black. Most of these beetles produced their own oil during the frying process which often spared us the trouble of adding any oil.

Edible Termites (*Ngobe*)

T here were three main types of edible termites in Alahtene. Some were collected after building a conical grass hut on top of the termites' hill. The process involved planting two wooden poles firmly into holes that led into the termites' underground habitat. Then several holes would be dug around the hut where the termites would fall when they came out to dance to the rhythm of the sounds produced from hitting the poles with smaller sticks. Sometimes, the insects came out because they were disturbed by the vibration of the implanted poles being struck with other sticks, accompanied by all-night singing.

Harvesting termites was a hard job that required a whole night's energy of singing and playing of sounds by striking the two wooden poles. The sweet musical sounds produced by the combination of strikes on the poles either excited or disturbed the termites from underneath their dwelling place. Consequently, they would rush out in their numbers and fall into the large holes that had been dug around the entrance to the grass hut. It needed at least two people to do the job and Ajuenekoh usually took me along. Those harvesting the termites must not fall asleep. They were expected to stay up all night, singing "termite songs" and striking the two poles with sticks to produce a dancing rhythm for the termites.

During one of our expeditions, I felt asleep and Ajuenekoh scolded: "go ahead and cover those small eyes of yours; tomorrow for your punishment, you will not eat any of the termites." Since I enjoyed fried termites a lot, I woke up suddenly and started singing the termite song: *mbuhngoh mah yamdeh, oh ho yamdeh, mbugoh loh te yueteh, eh eh yamdeh*. By early morning, we had collected more than two huge bags, each weighing over fifty kilograms. I couldn't believe my eyes. I was so happy that I would eat a lot of this delicacy and possibly, share some with my friends, if uncle did not monitor my moves. I also knew Ajuenekoh would make a lot of money selling most of the termites. I used to wonder what he really did with the money obtained from selling termites, fish, honey, wild animals etc.

The other type of edible termites called *ngoh bangie* was harvested during the rainy season during heavy downpour. The third type of termites were usually collected around four o'clock in the evening by covering their holes with baskets and some dry grass. It seems the termites always wanted to come out of the holes around that time and noticing that their holes had been covered, they would flock out in their numbers and end up being harvested instead. Termites were not only a reliable source of protein but also served as an income generating activity because they were sold to villagers. Humans were not the only ones interested in the termites. We observed that each time they came out, they would attract other creatures such as birds, toads and even snakes which ate them as food.

Grandmother was fond of telling us stories about the harvesting of termites. One of them concerned a character who left Alahtene to visit a distant village where the people's main occupation was harvesting termites. It happened that when the man, a notorious crook in Alahtene, arrived one of the homes where a huge quantity of termites had been harvested, he pretended to be a traveller on his way to the next village. Since it was already nightfall, he needed a place to spend the night and was offered accommodation by the homeowners. The kind hosts had harvested, fried and filled two big jute bags of termite which were ready for the market the next day. As custom demanded, the host offered the stranger some of the termites but he pretended and rejected the offer, stating that he could not eat insects that resembled little cockroaches. He bragged that in his hometown, no one would dare to eat those insects because they were considered nasty and meant for birds and toads. Before the homeowners retired to bed, they concerted among themselves whether it was wise to carry the bags of termites to another hidden spot within the house for fear the stranger could steal them at night. Most of them rejected the idea that the stranger would steal something he did not consume. So, they left the bags in the room where the stranger slept. When everybody had retired for the night, completely exhausted, the stranger stole the two heavy bags, each of which weighed about 50 kilos and travelled the whole night back to Alahtene. He eventually sold them for a lot of money.

The moral of the story, Ndih said, was that you should never trust strangers with your goods even if the stranger convinces you they don't consume the said product.

Edible Crickets (*Nchineh*)

These vegetable-eating large nocturnal insects were usually harvested as they came out of their holes at night, chirping (usually the males inviting the females to mate or eat the maize leaves, groundnuts and other vegetables). We hunted crickets by using lit pieces of wood or lamps filled with kerosene. We would trace the noise of the chirping male cricket and then use a cutlass to block off its hole. On hearing the noise caused by our movement, the cricket would seek to retreat to its hole but it would be too late. The blurring light and the fact that its hole was blocked would leave it helpless. Once captured, we would plug off its legs, then press its head to subdue it. Other edible crickets were also harvested when farming or weeding. A night's catch was enough protein to feed a house of three. Once we brought them home, we would plug off their wings, wash them and then fry them in an empty clay pot (without oil or water). The insects produced their own fat (oil). We would add a bit of salt and other spices until they were crispy and ready for consumption. Ndih also cherished them and her face would beam with a smile when she munched them with either plantains, sweet potatoes or pumpkins.

During my childhood, it was common to see freshly harvested or dried crickets skewered to bamboo sticks and sold at the village market. Sometimes, they were sold in baskets. Today, kids look down on the consumption of crickets and many other edible insects.

Harvesting Wild Honey

Harvesting wild honey was another fun activity during my stay at Ndih's house. During the day, Ajuenekoh would explore and establish the location of a beehive. He was so knowledgeable for his age. Upon inspecting the hive, he would tell if it had enough honey or not. At night he would make a torch light out of broken bamboo sticks tied together. He would then dress up in thick old clothes, his head fully covered in a bonnet and we'll set out, carrying either clay pots or big calabashes for the harvest. He usually avoided wearing red colours.

Upon locating the hive, (often around a tree trunk), Ajuenekoh would tiptoe to the beehive while I waited at a convenient distance with the lit bamboo torchlight. He would use some of the smoky bamboo sticks to frighten or weaken the bees. Often, the angry bees would leave the hive and head for the torchlight. My fear of bees was indescribable and on one occasion, I ran away with the torchlight in my hands, fell into a thick bush where I buried my face and head. Ajuenekoh almost burst out in laughter were it not for fear of being stung by the bees. This incident always reminded me of the story of a village kid who became dumb and deaf after a swarm of bees stung him almost to death. Were it not for the timely intervention of an adult who rescued and immersed him in a nearby river, the boy would have died. Consequently, I dreaded bees but loved their honey.

The night I escaped with the torchlight, Ajuenekoh harvested so much honey and suffered only a few bee stings. Some of the bees tried desperately to follow the honeycombs but our containers were tightly sealed. The morning after our harvest, I ate so much honey and then headed off to invite my friends to share. Ndih had a nickname for anyone who always invited everybody to see their catch/exploits "Mamanchoru". Each time I shared honey with my friends without Ajuenekoh's permission, he would punish me with insults that hurt my feelings: "look at her axe face, scattered teeth, etc." I hated it when anyone commented about the gap between my front teeth. When I grew up, I learned that among African women, being gap-toothed was considered beautiful.

Harvesting Red Soldier Ants' Eggs

Red soldier ants are a ferocious type of insects which attack, capture and eat other insects, animals and birds. They usually move like a great army in a colony and store their food or prey in a hole. When they bite, they would leave the spot only when their head has been cut off from their victim. In those days, their habitat was mostly found in the fields where they laid their eggs. My male peers had a good knowledge of the soldier ants' life cycle and precisely where to locate their small round white eggs which we all found highly nutritious. At an agreed time, our group would locate the ants' hole, dig deep and then use our bare hands to remove the eggs with such lightning speed before the ants could attack. We would pour our harvest into a basin, and then move to the next hole. By the time we were done, we would have a big basin of ants' egg which we would wash and fry (without oil), salt and eat them. Consuming the ants' eggs helped to reduce their population given that we did not have pesticides in the village. Another method to control them was to throw salt or wood ash on them but this was not often effective because they would come back at night to hunt for food.

Collecting the larvae of Palm Beetles (*Mbueh*)

Palm beetles are a species of insects whose larvae are highly cherished in Alahtene because of their high fat content. They usually entered the palm tree or raffia palm, ate up the interior and then made it their habitat and laid their larvae. Upon maturity, the beetle would break out from the tree and fly to another palm tree, leaving their larvae behind and the trees in a state of decay. To locate the larvae, we would inspect the raffia palms or fallen palm trees for traces of their presence. We would then dig through the tree and pick out the larvae which we fried and ate. We would also gift some to our uncles and aunts.

Typical house in Alahtene. This could easily be Ndih's house

Some of the fruit trees around Ndih's home include African plum trees. The ripe fruits are blueish in colour.

An old, rugged grinding machine similar to the first one in Alahtene

Alahtene market towards the evening during a Mbindo'o

Some types of foodstuffs prepared in grandmother's home: achu eaten with yellow soup, meat, vegetables, eggplant and egusi pudding

Fufu corn eaten with huckleberries (fufu corn and njama njama) with fried chicken

Pounded cocoyam fufu eaten with okra soup

Plantain porridge usually eaten as an entree.

Water fufu eaten with okra soup (obtained from fermented cassava)

Boiled groundnuts eaten like snacks usually with roasted fresh corn

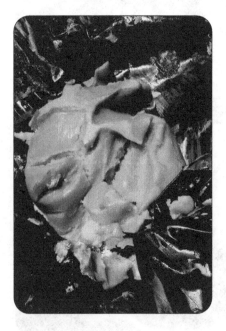

Koki beans (ground beans mixed with water and palm oil, tied in plantain leaves, and cooked by steaming) usually eaten with plantains, cocoyams, cassava) etc.

Roasted plums and fresh corn, usually eaten together

African plums roasted in a hot pot and eaten with cassava

Raffia palm wine being tapped

Raffia palm wine (sap) being served

Fruit pulp of the raffia tree. When ripe, it is boiled and eaten as a dessert/snack while drinking raffia palm wine. The hard nuts are used as ornaments for dancing and the seeds for propagation.

Ground berries from the wild (nejueh)

*Ripe Achoh harvested
from the wild*

Edible Mushrooms

A subspecies of mushrooms harvested from the wild

Another subspecies of mushroom harvested from the wild and being prepared for cooking or smoking

A bag full of green grasshoppers

Edible termites

Edible crickets, (nchineh) yet to be prepared for frying or roasting

Freshly harvested palm beetles' larvae

Roasted palm beetle larvae ready for consumption

Kids on errand with their bicycle rims

Children with their wooden bicycles waiting to transport goods

11

HUNTING AND FISHING

Hunting was a typical dry season activity in Alahbukum in general and Alahtene in particular. However, during the rainy season when the grass turned green, a type of hunting was done when some wild animals came out to eat the fresh grass. Almost every household had a hunting dog which was often better nourished than those described by Gerald Durrell in his book *The Bafut Beagles*.

In the dry season, hunting expeditions usually began by someone starting a fire in the fields. Because the fields were normally very dry, the fire would spread rapidly, and villagers would come out with fresh tree branches or palm fronds to put out the fire. Birds, grasshoppers, and other creatures such as snakes, tortoises, snails, etc., would try to escape from the scourging wildfires. My peers and I would be stationed at the edges of the field, clubs in hand, as we waited for the fleeing animals - giant rats, cane rats, hares, antelopes, and other sub-species of rats of various beautiful colours. We were expected to chase them with our clubs and we often succeeded to kill the unfortunate ones. Although the large snakes frightened us by raising their large heads, the older boys often chased and killed some. Most large snakes were eaten as delicacies after their heads and tails had been cut off. These parts were either thrown away or sold to traditional healers who used them to prepare remedies for various ailments and snake bites. Captured large snakes like boas were normally sent to the Palace of the Fon of Alahbukum. The snakes were customarily cooked after being properly spiced, then wrapped in plantain leaves and cooked by steaming. They tasted like chicken, and we cherished eating them. Each hunting expedition came to an end when the game had been equitably shared.

During one of those hunting expeditions, I narrowly escaped with my life. This happened when my friends and I dug a hole, convinced that a cane rat was hiding in there. When we were satisfied that we had dug deep enough, I put my hand in and touched what I thought was the tail of the animal. But I was reluctant to pull out the animal and my friends yelled at me for being chicken-hearted. So, a more courageous friend shoved me aside and inserted her hand deep into the hole and pulled out the animal by the tail. Behold, it was a large snake, a black mamba. We screamed in unison, and she dropped it in fright as we took to our heels. A group of boys who were nearby quickly rushed in our direction and chased after the black mamba amid shouts from the girls. Unfortunately, the scary creature escaped into the forest. Since that day, I swore to never put my hand into a hole with the intention to pull out an animal. Ndih was so frightened that evening when I recounted the incident to her. She advised me to refrain from digging or putting my hands into a hole because it was so dangerous and reserved for men.

After the bushes had been burnt, fresh green grass would

sprout and the fields would look like well mowed golf fields. Sometimes when the grass was still fresh and green, my team of adventurers would accompany the boys to hunt small game with spears and hunting dogs. It was during one of these expeditions that we caught Adamu, the yellow monkey that became my favourite pet. Its mother was lucky enough to have escaped our chase. Sometimes, the boys in our cohort would set out traps for various types of animals and birds. Some of the traps were made of iron, gum, sticks, and ropes. Sometimes, they would dig trenches as well. The set traps were inspected every morning and evening. Occasionally, stray dogs, or unaccompanied children would fall into these traps and would need adult intervention to rescue them.

Some of the animals that were frequently caught by the traps included bush fowls, owls, and parrots. Owls were considered birds of ill omen because they made frightening sounds at night. It was believed that some witches and wizards of Alahtene transformed themselves into owls at night. Consequently, Ndih never ate them, so I too refrained from eating them.

Parrots were highly coveted and boys would use a type of glue from a gum tree which they would place on the branches of palm trees using ripe palm nuts as bait to catch them. Since they were always captured alive, the parrots were often sold to tourists. I never saw anyone ate parrots and I wondered why, until someone told me that parrots could say "please don't kill me" in the Alahtene language. This explains why no one ate parrots. However, I later learned that parrots from our part of the world were very intelligent and could mimic several words even in English. Eventually, wildlife officers later prohibited the commercialization of parrots because they had become an endangered species. Despite this, the illegal capture and sale of parrots still goes on in Alahtene till date.

Adult hunting involved the use of dogs wearing bells on their necks, spears and sometimes Dane guns. During hunting expeditions, the hunters would encourage their dogs by promising to give them the intestines of the captured game. The adult hunters frequently caught cane rats, antelopes, deer and monkeys and on rare occasions, big birds.

It happened that once upon a time, a large species of birds invaded the village. Hunters announced the bad news and stated that they had been spotted in another distant village. The birds were reported to have preyed on young babies, so all baby-sitters were warned not to leave babies unsupervised or securely harnessed. News about the birds had hardly circulated when they arrived our village. It was thought to have been a species of vultures.

All professional hunters in Alahtene set out, well-armed with guns to the forests where the birds had sought temporary habitat. When the hunters finally spotted the birds they shot at them but one of the wounded vultures unexpectedly attacked a hunter, who, in his attempt to retreat, slipped on the muddy surface and fell. It is recounted that were it not for the bravery and timely intervention of the other hunters who ran to the man's rescue by firing more gunshots at the wounded bird, the situation could have been different. It was only then that the beast finally fell and its companions flew away and never returned to the village. Four hefty hunters carried the bird on their shoulders tied on two large, long poles and brought it to the village. The carcass of the bird was laid in the market square and the entire village came out to see. Nobody would dare eat the carnivorous bird which measured about four feet wide. It was later taken to the palace of the king of Alahbukum. We later learnt that the bird's carcass had been used for traditional medicine to deter such "witches" from ever visiting any of the villages in the kingdom again.

Another incident that seriously endangered the lives of several hunters involved the killing of a baby gorilla. Two of the brave hunters had gone to a gorilla habitat and saw a mother gorilla nursing her babe on a treetop. When one of them sighted the mammal and was about to shoot it with his gun, the mother gorilla allegedly lifted her hands and pleaded to the hunter for mercy, pointing to her breast. The second hunter advised his companion to spare the animal because it was a nursing mother. The stubborn hunter refused and without delay, shot at the gorilla but the bullet missed the mother and killed the babe instead. The angry animal jumped to the ground and realised that its baby was dead. She lifted the young animal, placed it on her chest and noticed that it was not breathing. She belched and charged towards the hunter who by now had taken off. Mother gorilla quickly caught up with the fleeing hunter, snatched his gun, broke it into pieces and pounced on the man. She hit him so hard that he fell to the ground and pretended that he was dead by laying there motionless. His companion had hidden himself behind some trees in the forest, observing the events as they unfolded. Once the gorilla thought the hunter was dead, it returned to its babe and howled. Within a short time, all the male gorillas came running to the spot and surrounded the dead young animal. They all mourned just like humans in Alahtene did. Then the bereaved mother took the rest of the group to show them where it had beaten the hunter. Fortunately for the hunter, his friend had come to his rescue, and they had both returned to the village where they recounted their misadventure. Ndih always reminded me that gorillas and chimpanzees were just like humans, hence, the reason why she never ate their meat. Since hearing this story, I promised myself never to eat the flesh of any great ape and to become their protector one day.

The Last Elephant is Killed

Compared to other animals in Alahtene, elephants were uncommon. Although they were known to always move in a herd, it happened that one day, an elephant strayed into the village. The young hunters who identified it quickly rushed back to report the matter to the villagers. The strayed animal was eating elephant grass stalk which grew in abundance in Alahtene. Unfortunately, it also ate everything green on its path and destroyed farms and crops. On hearing the news, the town crier sounded the alarm on his buffalo horn, which could be heard more than eight miles away. The message was clear to the villagers - there was imminent attack on the village. Every young man and adult male came out with their spears and Dane guns and assembled at the village head's residence. The women also joined them, curious to find out why everyone had been summoned so suddenly. The news was that an elephant had been spotted which ought to be killed, otherwise it would destroy crops and houses and possibly kill people. The frightened women gave the men their full blessings and the protection of Alahbukum's ancestors.

The men, who numbered over a hundred took off, tracing the animal's tracks. After about two miles, they found the animal standing under a baobab tree. Immediately, the chase began as the men threw their spears at the poor creature while singing war songs. The elephant ran towards the hills while enduring the sharp piercing of the spears that rained on its body. When the men had exhausted their spears, those with Dane guns took over and began to shoot. Just before they ran out of gun powder, the animal collapsed from exhaustion and loss of blood near the top of the hill. It had been running for more than three hours.

The men rushed to the fallen mammal, removed their sharp hunting knives, cutlasses, short axes from their raffia bags and started chopping the panting elephant's thick flesh. Some men cut off branches of trees and quickly wove large bags with which to carry the animal's parts. Every bit of the animal was sliced into portable portions and transported to Chief Elder's compound where it was to be distributed among the hunters. Its tusks, tail and heart were immediately taken to the King of Alahbukum's palace. What remained of the elephant was then shared amongst everyone who was part of the expedition.

This incident happened during the second year spent with my grandmother. It was also the year I was in Infants Two. In those days, animals like the elephant and other endangered species were not protected. This was also the first time I tasted elephant meat because my uncle Ajuenekoh was part of the hunting team. Regrettably, that was also the last elephant ever spotted in Alahtene.

Cooking elephant meat consumed a considerable amount of our firewood because it was so tough and produced a lot of fat. We drained the fat and kept it for frying ripe plantains, potatoes and vegetables. My grandmother refused to taste the elephant meat when it was ready. Ndih said that elephants were not edible because their flesh was made up of all types of other animals' flesh.

Following this incident, women of Alahtene composed one of the most popular songs of that era - an elephant song in which they praised the men and youth for their bravery in killing such a huge animal. The king of Alahbukum sent a team of notables to decorate those who had taken part in killing the animal. As we grew up and remembered this incident, I resolved that when I would become a lawyer or judge, I would protect elephants and other wildlife species from extinction.

Depletion of other Wildlife Species

It was common for some hunters in Alahtene to go hunting for weeks. While in the forest, they would build small huts as shelter for the duration of their stay. It was also inside these huts that they would smoke their game which included bush fowls, boars, deer, antelopes, cane rats and porcupines. Ndih once recounted the story about one of those great hunters who, having stayed in the forest for over a week, returned home carrying a large bag full of bushmeat. However, he was so hungry upon his arrival that he immediately requested his two wives to prepare him a meal as fast as possible. By the time the women brought the delicious meal – corn fufu and okra soup with egusi, dried meat and fresh spices - he was too tired to eat by himself, so he asked to be fed. The two women obliged, and he swallowed the soft corn paste at such lightning speed with no time to utter a word. When he was done eating, he was given a calabash of freshly tapped raffia palm wine which he gulped without breaking. When his wives retired to their respective houses, he was left without company, unable to move or talk. It wasn't until one of his sons returned from his farm and came to greet him that he discovered his dad's state. The man simply whistled "whoeh hu huhu!" Unable to decipher what he was trying to communicate, the poor man ended up simply pointing to his inflated stomach and specifically the belt under his belly. The boy quickly searched for a sharp knife with which he cut off the girdle, thereby freeing his father to breathe properly. The hunter's son later shared the story with his mother and it eventually spread throughout the village. Henceforth, when kids saw the hunter passing by, they would whistle the desperate sound in mockery.

Bushmeat was highly cherished by all and available for sale on most market days. They included monkeys, deer, buffalo, porcupines, bush fowls, wild boars, antelopes, etc. The high demand for bushmeat and the fact that hunting was not regulated eventually led to the depletion and extinction of some of the animal species.

Fishing

Fishing was another major seasonal activity. One of the senior girls, a daughter of Ndih's friend, Mah Mabifor was charged with the task of teaching me how to fish. First, we wove two kinds of fishing baskets - a large open and long basket used for catching the fish and a smaller one with a lid which we tied around our waist. Each time we went fishing, we would set out early in the morning when fishes were expected to come out of their hiding spots to look for food. We would put a variety of herbs in the large fishing baskets and tiptoe into the stream especially in the deep areas. There, we would quietly place the baskets for a few minutes and then pull it out very swiftly. Fish that had entered the basket to eat the herbs would be trapped and caught. We would repeat this pattern throughout the morning while moving upstream. Our regular catch included big and small crabs, big and small fishes and big frogs. My trainer would squeeze the frogs' intestines through their mouths which killed them instantly. For the fish, we would press their heads before putting them in the smaller baskets with the lids.

After each fishing trip, Ndih would tell me a story that had an important lesson. One of them involved a woman called Ngwe who had a big impending event and needed fish, meat, food and palm wine. One early morning, she embarked on a solo fishing expedition where she spent many hours catching a variety of fishes from the river until her big basket was full to the brim. On her way back, her basket carefully balanced on her head, she spotted a deer under the cool shade of a large tree probably resting from the scorching sun. Somehow, she imagined it was a dead animal. So, she began to wonder aloud how she would transport the deer given that her basket was already full of fish. She was convinced that it was her luckiest day. After evaluating her options, she resolved to return to the river and emptied her basket's contents and then hastened back to the spot where she found the deer. Finding the animal in the same spot, she burst into song and began to dance around the animal: "Ngwe's ceremony's preparations have succeeded, only palm wine is lacking now!" She sang and danced, circling the animal several times. Finally, she bent over to pick up the animal by its leg, but it kicked and rose to its feet, seemingly confused, and then ran off at lightning speed.

Shocked and confused herself, the woman fell to the ground and burst into tears. She gathered courage and ran back to the river hoping to find the fish still floating on top of the water but to her greatest dismay, they were all gone. She carried her hands on her head in desperation and wept bitterly as she returned to the village where she recounted the story of her own stupidity. News of her foolishness spread rapidly throughout the village and thus, she became the subject of a popular song around drinking places.

This story taught its listeners a beautiful lesson about the importance of being careful in decision making because if the woman had thrown her fish under the tree, she could have recovered them after failing to catch the deer. Also, had she found out if it were a sleeping or dead deer, she would have spared herself the folly that ensued. "A bird in hand is worth two in the bush", the proverb says.

I enjoyed fishing with friends until one day we encountered a long snake in the stream, and we fled from the waters, completely frightened. This incident frightened me so badly that I stopped fishing with my friends.

Another fishing technique involved placing large baskets filled with herbs on the stream bed in the evening and then checking their contents early in the morning or evening the next day. The catch - fish, crabs, tadpoles, frogs etc., were usually smoked and used for preparing various soups, especially black soup for achu.

Ajuenekoh and his friends would fish with hooks, using earth worms as baits. They frequently caught mud fish or catfish which they sold. They also used some of their income to play checkers and to rent bicycles which they rode around with joy. This was an upgrade from using the rims of abandoned bicycle wheels or self-fabricated wooden bikes which frequently accompanied them on errands.

12

ENTERTAINMENT AT NDIH'S

A popular pastime amongst the older boys and girls was story telling. Participants were expected to compete in telling the funniest story, riddles or rhymes. They were also expected to keep a straight face while striving to evoke as much laughter out of listeners as possible. Another category included a storytelling contest that included a song. Stories were usually told around the fireside while eating boiled groundnuts and roasted corn.

The longest story I ever heard was "Give me back my belongings". This story involved a mischievous boy who was always kind to people, giving them assistance whenever they were in need, but would in turn request the assisted person to return the donated item. It was frequently the case that the person would have already used it or consumed it and the mischievous boy would oblige the person to replace the item with something better. He became notorious for embarrassing people until one day, he ended up receiving a spear because that was the only item the person had. The returned spear was however inferior to the item he had initially given to the beneficiary.

There were many stories notably about the tortoise who won long distance races by claiming that it did not like to run on the main road but preferred the bushes. Once that rule was accepted, tortoise forged a plan by stationing its friend near the finish line. Once the whistle was blown, the tortoise would take off at the starting point along with the other animals while spectators cheered them on. However, tortoise's friend stationed near the finish line would simply crawl out of its hiding spot and cross the finish line as winner while panting. The lion, deer and antelope would protest in disappointment and anger, but the tortoise was always declared winner by the judges. Because all tortoises resembled each other, it was a challenge to prove that the victorious tortoise wasn't the same one that began the race with the other animals. This is how the tortoise always emerged as the winner in long-distance races.

Another story about tortoise's adventures included an account of why he always won the contest for the position of "king of the animal world". In this story, the tortoise was the only traditional healer in his village and all other animals had to seek treatment with him when they fell sick. Each time a sick animal came for consultation, he would arrange with his wife to tell them that he was out running some important errands. Mrs. Tortoise would tell them to return later. Upon their return, they would find Mr. Tortoise at home, pretending to be sick and unable to walk. Desperate for his services, the animals would be obliged to carry him to their residence so he could treat the sick animal. Just before their arrival at the patient's home, the tortoise would pull out a cane which he always carried around concealed and whip the animal transporting him. He would then declare to the assembly of animals gathered at the patient's home (whom he had secretly invited): "if I told you all that I am king of all the wild animals, you wouldn't have believed me but here I am being carried. All of you should hail me and say "Mr. Tortoise is king of all the animals and can ride on the back of any animal when he wants." All the animals obliged but the lion protested "the tortoise can't be the king of the wild animals for, I, lion, am king! I am the strongest!"

Not long after this incident, the powerful lion was humiliated by the same tortoise when he came to consult on behalf of his sick wife. Prior to the lion's arrival, tortoise had extracted and drunk the juice of garden huckleberry seeds (the extract looked like dark blood). When the lion arrived, the tortoise claimed he too was sick and might even die. As he spoke, he vomited the thick blood-like liquid, and the lion was moved by pity at tortoise's condition. Mr. Lion had no choice but to carry Mr. Tortoise on its back so that he could diagnose and treat his wife, Mrs. Lioness. Upon arrival at the lion's den where all the other animals had been summoned by the tortoise, the latter reached for his hidden cane and started whipping the lion, declaring that he, the tortoise was the "king of all the animals". The evidence, he declared, was available for all to see – the lion himself had carried him on his back. The lion felt embarrassed and ashamed because he had only carried the tortoise on his back because he thought the cunning animal was indeed ill. To make up for humiliating the lion, the tortoise treated Mrs. Lioness without any charge, but the lion's pride had been severely wounded. While tortoise could whip all the animals and get away with it, he in turn could not be whipped because he would recoil into his shell if any of the animals dared to beat him.

There is also the story of how the tortoise treated the pig so poorly. Each time the pig visited the tortoise to reclaim money he had loaned him, Mr. Tortoise would immediately turn his back and ask his wife to use him as a grinding stone. She would tell the pig that her husband had gone out on errands. Each time there was a knock at the door, tortoise's wife would inquire who it was. If the pig responded that he was the one, Mr. Tortoise would turn his back so that his wife would use him as a grinding stone. The pig eventually got fed up with his daily visits and not finding the tortoise at home. He also could not figure out why Mrs. Tortoise was always grinding stuff each time he visited. He threatened to throw away Mrs. Tortoise's grinding stone if he found her still grinding stuff the next day. Predictably, he returned as planned and without finding Mr. Tortoise, seized his wife's grinding stone and threw it far into the bush. The morning after he threw away the grinding stone, he returned to reclaim his money and found Mr. Tortoise at home. The tortoise told Mr. Pig that he had the money to repay his debt, but he would only do so on condition that he returned his wife's grinding stone. The pig went out to the spot where he had thrown the stone but couldn't find it. Since that day, Mr. Pig and his friends always dig the earth, hoping to find the lost grinding stone.

Ajeunekoh and his friends frequently joined us in storytelling. However, their own stories were always full of horror and action just like in horror movies. What amazed us was that they themselves were often characters in their stories who allegedly saw ghosts at night. One category of ghosts consisted of giant human-like creatures with super long legs who walked about with their heads touching the dark night sky. These creatures were often found at crossroads where they terrorized humans, especially young people who went out at night. They called this category of ghosts *Darkness*. These ghosts were notorious for using their long legs to kick anyone walking around at night. No human would dare engage them in combat because a solid kick could crush any human.

Another category of ghosts was known as *imps*. They always carried whips and took pleasure in whipping young children who dared to move about at night. They also moved about as a gang and frequently attacked young men of Ajeunekoh's age. Despite their miniature sizes, the *imps* always succeeded to beat the young men who always fled for their dear lives. *Imps*, the bigger boys claimed, had acrobatic skills, could jump high into the air and could chase their victims at lightning speed.

My uncle and his friends also told scary tales about pythons that swallowed their victims. That was why they always went about carrying razor blades or sharp knives in their pockets. Should they be swallowed by a python, they would easily free themselves by cutting through the beast's stomach. In fact, most of them even claimed that they had been swallowed by pythons (although no one had witnessed it) and they had freed themselves by using their blades. We were terrified by these stories and sometimes had nightmares about these terrifying creatures. If Ndih was around when Ajeunekoh and his friends recounted their tales, she would rebuke and declare them "tall tales".

During one of the storytelling sessions, Ndih claimed that she herself had seen a ghost. She was about fifteen then. She and her friends had decided to attend the moon dance at one of the compounds in the village. However, her mom had delayed her departure by asking her to complete some chores before leaving. By the time she was done, it was late and her mates had already gone ahead. By no means would she miss the dance, so she set off alone at night although the moon was bright. After a few minutes, she saw one of their neighbours who had been very ill walking ahead of her. Comforted by the prospects of having a companion, she called out to him saying "Tah, have you already recovered from your sickness? Please, wait for me to walk with you." The man did not answer, so she kept calling out for him to slow down as she tried to increase her pace. The man kept on walking and seemed to increase his steps. Her attempts to catch up with him failed until he branched off a side road. Ndih continued her lonely walk, wondering about the neighbour's odd conduct until she arrived at the moon dance. There, she learned the neighbour she had seen had died earlier that evening and that his corpse was still lying at his home. Ndih then recounted her odd experience with the "deceased" man.

When she returned home that night, she fell seriously ill. It took the intervention of a traditional doctor for her to regain her health. The doctor claimed Ndih was lucky she had survived because she had interacted with a ghost en route to the next world. Ndih's story sealed our belief that ghosts indeed existed and reinforced our fear to go about at night unless we were accompanied by adults. When I look back now, I ask myself if Ndih really saw a ghost. She was moving behind this fellow at night although with some moonlight; how sure was she that the man he saw was really their neighbour?

Alahbukum's capital was called Nsanimunwi which means god's child's playground. Folklore has it that the name was derived from an event that happened a very long time ago, soon after the forefathers of Alahbukum arrived their present site. They had crossed mountains, fertile plains, rivers and had waged battles with many groups before settling in Alahbukum.

They had erected the present palace after abandoning the old one that was in a hilly, remote village. One early morning on that ill-fated day, the population woke up and discovered the corpse of a beautiful little girl of about eight or nine, clothed in gold. She had golden beads on her plaited hair and waist, golden rings of various shades on her ankles, toes, fingers and nose. By every indication, she had fallen flat on her face from the skies. She did not resemble any of the local children and the strange golden basket in her hands contained objects never seen before in Alahbukum. A crowd soon gathered around the alien and word quickly reached the king's palace. Kwifor, the regulatory body of the kingdom was immediately dispatched to consult an oracle about the origins of the strange girl. The oracle reported that the girl had fallen to earth from another planet. It claimed she was a princess who had been sent on an errand to throw away trash in a pit. The curious little girl had peeped inside the pit and had suffered the misfortune of falling on planet earth. That she had landed near the king's palace, claimed the oracle, was not an accident. It was interpreted as a warning to the royals to be careful, otherwise a calamity would befall the royal children. The beautiful alien princess was consequently buried in that area following several rituals. The day after her burial, the Kwifor went out to the sacred waterfall to appease their gods by preparing a mixture of special herbs with the blood of a sacrificed goat as they chanted solemn songs to their ancestors, seeking their protection. This is the story behind the origin of the name Nsanimunwi which has been known as such until this day.

Other popular stories included kind but poor orphaned children who later became kings in foreign lands because of their humility, hard work and honesty. One of them concerned

"Sense Pass King" who inherited part of a large kingdom because the king had promised that anybody who would demonstrate exceptional intelligence and skills would inherit part of his kingdom and marry his daughter. In this story, Sense was tested by completing several difficult tasks; he had to shave the king's hair, spend time in detention in a mosquito infested area without killing or hitting any of them; eat the most spiced pepper soup without crying out "ash, ashu, ashu" (the sound produced by locals when they ate a very spicy dish). The intelligent but poor boy successfully completed all the hurdles. When he arrived to shave the king's hair, he brought along a cob of roasted fresh corn and told the king that where he came from, it was customary to eat roasted corn while shaving the hair of a very important personality like the king. When he was done, the king requested that Sense should collect and return the shaved hair to his head. Sense replied humbly: "Your royal majesty, since you are the king and everybody must follow your example, please, first put back the grains of the roasted sweet corn to their original lines on the cob." Unable to do this, the king withdrew his request and commanded the poor intelligent young man to move on to the next round of the competition.

The next challenge was for Sense to spend time with minimal clothing in a mosquito infested environment without hitting any of them off his body. Sense hatched a plan by composing a song for the king and his audience. His song went as such: "His royal majesty, when I was at the war front, bullets would come from this direction and enter my body through that direction (slaps his thigh that had just been bitten by mosquitoes), and went out this way, (slaps the mosquitoes behind his thighs), then some bullets would pierce his arms and come out at the back; some would hit his jaw and come out on the other side; bullets would enter here and come out that way, there, here, all over his body (slapping the various parts where mosquitoes had bitten him, his palms bloody). Amazed by his intelligence, the king asked Sense, "if all these bullets really entered your body, how come you didn't die?" Sense responded promptly "because I ate the pepper soup, and I was made by the gods to marry the king's daughter." The entire audience cheered for Sense and wondered how he had survived the mosquitoes' bites without hitting them. He was declared to have won a test many before him had failed and thus promoted to the third contest.

A pot of hot spicy pepper soup was brought, prepared from the hottest spices in Alahbukum (ginger, garlic, hot red, hot yellow, hot black and hot green peppers, several leafy spices). Sense was placed in a smoky room in the king's palace where he was expected to consume the pot of soup without producing the "ash" sound. Sense composed and sang another song "His majesty the king, remember I told you that when I was at the war front, the *Akamachu* (Military Captain) gave me this same kind of soup when the bullets entered all over my body. He gave the command to me, "when you eat this soup do not make the sound *ashu, ashu, ashu*"! When I ate the hot spicy soup, I never made the *ashu, ashu, ashuuuuu* sound but all my colleagues in the army who were with me, when they ate the same soup, they started saying *ashu, ashuu, ashuu* and the captain became angry and punished all those who made the sound "*ashu, ashuuu*". He removed them from the healing room because they made the sound "ashuuuuuuuuuuuuuuu"; that's why their own bullet wounds did not get healed and they all died because they made the sound ashuuuuuuuuuu after eating the hot spicy pepper soup. One of the reasons I was healed was because I never made the sound "ashuuuuuuuuuuuu". When the set time for the contest expired and the judges having stepped out, the king, feeling the effects of the spices in his eyes and nostrils, declared Sense the winner. Sense had outsmarted his fellow contestants and was thus permitted to marry the princess. A portion of the kingdom was given him to rule, and he started teaching young people how to apply their intelligence in getting things done. His new name became Sense Pass King.

Other stories involved ghosts and extra-terrestrial beings called "little men". Ghosts were known to haunt criminals and when they chased their targets, they always outpaced them. One evening, when stories about these ghosts were being told, a kid who had been listening, eventually fell asleep in one of the beds in Ndih's house. While he slept, a bunch of corn poorly fastened fell from the ceiling on to the boy, so he jumped out of bed and began to scream the name of the ghost "*nkuwah, nkuwah, achuameghah*" meaning "oh dear, oh dear, the ghost, the ghost has caught me". There was great commotion as other children all rushed from their beds towards Ndih's side of the room. Ndih laughed and reassured them that none of the so-called ghosts would ever dare come near any of her grandchildren because all the kids were good boys and girls.

Besides stories, we also entertained each other with riddles. Some of them included the following: "there are many crabs in a river and only one fish"; the answer is the teeth and one's tongue; "someone who usually stands on a hilltop and boasts to death"; the answer is a cricket chirping at night (whose sound usually invited people to kill it for food; "so many breasts pushing out in the wild"; the answer is mushroom, etc. Our storytelling sessions usually lasted late into the night which by village standards could be about 11 p.m.

At grandmother's place, every child had a voice. During the storytelling episodes, each child narrated their story, embellished it, received input and answered questions from their peers. Grandmother would correct the way the stories were told and summarize the lessons learned. In her own manner, she was training future leaders and orators.

Moon Dancing

The bright moonlight in the night sky presented another exciting moment at Ndih's home for a popular activity – moon dancing also called *asseme*. Ndih told us stories how dancing in the moonlight during her time could attract "goddesses" who descended to dance with humans. It was alleged that when these goddesses danced, their feet and toes did not touch the ground and they did not chat with other children. This story never deterred any of us from dancing in the moon. The dance usually started with less than ten children and as the sound and rhythms of the songs grew louder, more people would join. The songs usually praised the beauty of the moon and appealed for its brightness to last longer; that children and even kings loved the moon; that it was the ideal time to be happy… etc. During the dance, a big circle would be formed, and each person would occupy the centre for a period, displaying his or her dancing styles; then she or he would invite another dancer to the centre where they would dance together for a while and then the invited person would take over in the middle, displaying his or her dance moves. The moon dance was a great opportunity for local kids to learn how to dance to the rhythm of traditional music.

Folk Music and Dance

Every large family had its own distinct dance troupe commanded by the family or compound head. Each family rehearsed their songs at reunions when members met to *fehnekwap* – that is, to discuss a family issue intended to avoid misfortune from befalling a member, celebrations of *ndahmooh* - a new birth, marriage, or title obtained from the palace. Such rehearsals usually increased in frequency leading up to the Fon's Annual Dance known as *Abin e Mfor.*

The week before this royal dance, the population would be busy watching various performances as dancers competed for the title of top dancer. The troupe selected by the elders as the best was normally expected to represent the whole village at the fon's dance. In addition, the rest of the village was expected to practice the moves of the selected or winning troupe, and every Alahtene citizen proudly performed it at the annual dance with much fanfare. Some of the items that were given out as prizes after the dance included decorated calabashes, carved buffalo horns, woven traditional bags and many other highly valued items.

Music Instruments

The instruments used in traditional dances in Alahtene were of various shapes, sizes and origins. They included the buffalo horns, xylophones, drums of various sizes and colours, flutes made from Indian bamboos, two-way flutes called *mandere* made from iron rods; several iron-made round objects bent at the edges, big heavy clay pots with tiny elongated mouths which were played by striking a soft sponge against the hollow mouth; decorated calabashes tucked with dried shells from the wild African bush butter tree; woven raffia patches worn on the arms and legs, slightly dug wooden tree trunks played with small iron rods embellished with beads from the savanna spear grass. Frequently, masked dancers would also perform, wearing wooden frightful masks on their heads which covered their faces; they also dressed up in clothes made of feathers, raffia palm fiber, tree bark, and sometimes woven raw cotton. Female dancers usually wore very bright colours - *cha cha* skirts and tied their breast with a piece of cloth, coloured their faces with camwood or white chalk clay.

I was always amazed each time I watched various dance groups displaying their artistic talents and rhythms. It was fascinating to learn that every single village troupe in Ndih's days could transform anything into a musical instrument and it was always engaging to watch or listen to the sounds and rhythms produced by their instruments.

13

NDIH'S "COURT"

Many cases were judged by my grandmother in her capacity as a female member of the council of elders. One of the cases she had to mediate late into the night concerned two families that had a dispute over the custody of a little girl of about five. Each group had sought to pull the child into their camp and the little girl, overwhelmed by the situation, burst into tears. A woman who heard the girl's cry dashed off to report the matter to Ndih. Fortunately, Ajuenekoh and his peers were present, so, Ndih sent them to bring the disputing parties. When they arrived Ndih's home, visibly angry, she calmed them down and then sought to understand why they were trying to tear the child into pieces. Each party claimed the little girl was theirs, so Ndih asked them to state their case. The first family to explain their case claimed that the little girl's mother was their late brother's wife and that when their brother died, the girl's mother had refused to marry the late man's dad. She had also decided to run away from the home she shared with her late husband, which incidentally was located within the same compound as her father-in-law's. When she left her marital residence, she had taken her daughter along with her, but her in-laws had abducted the little girl from her maternal grandmother's home where she was being kept in secret. The widow's relatives in due course, returned and kidnapped the little girl but were intercepted by her paternal relatives.

Having listened attentively to each party's explanation, Ndih expressed her disgust at the scenario, expressing herself in proverbs "a house where there is no peace cannot raise a child; children always die in such homes; that trying to tear the little girl to pieces was already bad enough and that exchanging such angry words in the presence of a small child late at night was equally bad enough; doing such things was tantamount to inviting evil spirits to afflict the child, thus jeopardizing her destiny." She reprimanded the two parties for not recognising the damage they were doing to the kid. Never in the history of the clan had she heard that a widow could marry her father-in-law. Tradition permitted a widow to marry her brother-in-law but, in this case, no direct brother-in-law had been available, hence, the widow's decision to run away. She advised the kid's paternal relatives to permit her maternal relatives to raise her. She would eventually seek her father's relatives when she grows up. Meanwhile, the child's paternal relatives must continue to play their role by providing for the child's upkeep. When Ndih gave her verdict, the big boys cheered and Ndih simply smiled. The little girl had long fallen asleep. That was the night I resolved I would study law and become a judge when I grow up.

When we woke up the next morning, I asked Ndih why those two families were so angry at each other. Ndih responded in proverbs, "those people are like a type of locust which attacked this village once and when the locust had finished eating every plant leaf, and since the villagers hid all their goats, cow and hens in covered shelters, the locusts began to eat one another." She said due to poverty, both families were not seeking the child's best interest but rather, were interested in what would bring them material gain over the child's custody.

The Woman Behind the Bushes with Three Kids

Another case that was brought to Ndih for mediation occurred early one morning and concerned a young mother with her three kids (two of whom could walk and the youngest on her back), accused by her mother-in-law for trying to escape from her marital home. According to the young woman's mother-in-law, she had gone to collect her debt from a villager and was on her way back when she heard one of her grandkids calling out to her from the bushes, "grandma, grandma, here we are, hiding". The grandmother said she recognised her eldest grandson's voice and shouted in return, "Musseuh, why are you hiding in the bush early in the morning?" However, the child did not respond. Frightened, she started moving in the direction where she heard her grandson's voice. She was startled to find her daughter-in-law with her children hiding in the bushes behind a tree along with a few of her belongings. She asked them why they were hiding and one of the children said they were running away from the house. The grandmother exclaimed and alerted everyone to see what was happening. This infuriated the daughter-in-law who burst into tears without saying a word. People soon appeared at the scene and the grandmother took the children and their mother to Ndih's house. She asked Ndih to help her find out why her daughter-in-law was trying to run away from her marital home. After sobbing for a while, the woman recollected herself and said she sought to run away because her husband was maltreating her. She said her husband (a prince) was interested in marrying more wives rather than providing for the basic needs of the one he already had. On market days, she claimed, he would spend all their savings on drinks and hardly brought home essential groceries like meat or other necessities like soap, cooking oil and kerosene. She said she was tired of fending for herself, and children and would prefer to return to her parents. Instead of comforting her, the mother in-law told her she was free to leave but she had no right to take her children along with her. She didn't bring the children with her into the marriage, claimed the grandmother. I sat pretentiously as if I was busy doing something, but I listened attentively and felt angry at the mother-in-law's words.

Ndih counselled the woman's mother-in-law, stating she had a right to be angry if she was not well treated by her husband whom Ndih classified as a drunkard. Ndih told the children's grandmother that if she had daughters of her own, she would have been more sensitive and would love to see that they are well treated by their husbands. Ndih advised the grandmother to call her son to order and required that they should return in two weeks' time for her to evaluate if their situation had improved. She also required that the lady's husband must purchase new wax print cloth as a show of remorse for his poor behaviour to her. Two weeks later, the pair returned to Ndih's house, and the younger woman was beaming with joy and thanked Ndih for her wisdom.

When the young woman later delivered a baby girl, she named the child after Ndih Maghrebong, as an expression of her appreciation for saving her marriage. Ndih's sense of fairness in judgement became legendary and many of the grandmothers in Alahtene who had previously supported their sons' wrongdoings to their wives, began to heed to Ndih's counsel.

Rivalry between Neighbouring Kids

It was not customary for kids in Alahtene to allow other kids to utter their parents' name especially their fathers'. It was common for kids to insult each other by yelling out their parents' names. One day, our neighbours' children (six kids), who resided on the left of Ndih's house launched an attack on us when one of my cousins visited me. This happened when we went to fetch water from the nearby stream and the kids started by calling my dad's names and I boldly told them not to call my father's name. They continued, so in retaliation my cousin and I also called their father's names without the honorific "tah". The kids started chanting and dancing to the tune of my own father's name, so we responded in like manner.

The overwhelming shouts of our adversaries created a great negative influence on my cousin who became confused and joined their camp in chanting my dad's name "*Atimooh, oh, atimoh oh, atimooh*". I burst into tears because I considered my cousin's defection's a big blow for me. This enabled our neighbour's kids to claim victory. When we went home and recounted the incident to Ndih, she laughed and said calling one's father's name did not subtract or add anything to his status and that it was because my father was important that people loved calling his name. She said, at best it was jealousy. By the way, she added, their father was a tapper of raffia palm wine. However, I knew that our neighbour's raffia palm wine was highly appreciated and bought by many people so he must be a wealthy man – so why would his children be jealous of my father? Whatever the case, I learnt a new lesson – to ignore people and not get angry when people called my dad's names.

In most neighbourhoods, kids participated in many play-ful activities that provoked laughter, fights, and tears. It was also remarkable that parents hardly intervened in children's quarrels. Should a fight break out and news of this got to the parents, the issue was resolved by tasking those involved to fetch water from the stream, fetch firewood or clear a portion of farmland. Because of this penalty, many kids refrained from reporting their squabbles to their parents.

Commerce and Saving

At Ndih's home we produced most of our own foodstuffs except rice, which we ate on special occasions like Christ-mas and New Year's Day. On local market days, I would sell palm kernels, cooked raffia palm nuts (*akuh*), bananas and/or roasted groundnuts. Every month, my friends and I would go to Aghahsah where the town market was located, about ten kilometres from Alahtene. The journey was even more tedious because we had to transport our market items on our heads. At the market, we sometimes sold green vegetables and raw groundnuts. During the dry season, we would sell firewood. Upon arrival at the market, our produce was often bought by the town ladies, who were often well dressed and wore fancy shoes. After selling our items, my friends and I would buy *mai-mai* for breakfast - a delicious pudding made from ground beans, cooked in tins. It was only sold in big towns like Aghah-sah. The town's main commercial district was called Wabaka. We also bought a type of snack made from groundnut paste called *kurukuru*. Ndih didn't like it because it was too hard for her to chew. Some of her teeth had fallen off but she ate a bit just to please me because I always boasted how delicious it tasted. I was always so happy when she accepted to taste any of the snacks I loved.

From the money I got after selling my items, I would buy some palm oil, beef, crayfish and salt with which we spiced our smoked mushroom soup, crab soup or porridge. I also always bought kerosene and hid the balance somewhere safe, known only to Ndih and I. Ajuenekoh and his friends were never to be trusted

To ease the tedious journey back home, we would devise games along the way. One of them involved assigning lucky numbers to each member of our team and if a passing car had the corresponding number, we would award the number holder a point.

There was a specific spot under Ndih's bamboo bed where we hid all our money, tied in a piece of black cloth. I always knew the amount of money we had in the secret safe. Occasionally, some of Ndih's young female friends in dire need of money would come to borrow money from her. She would ask the reason for the loan and if she found that reason convincing, she would ask the person to return at a stipulated time to get the money. This permitted us to remove the money from our safe and have it handy for the borrower. The ladies were always so grateful to Ndih Maghrebong. What would they do without her? They would say as they expressed their gratitude. It was also remarkable that her debtors always paid back the money on the promised date. Ndih could be considered a rich woman by local standards. From her, I learned very early in life the importance of saving money to avoid borrowing from people like some of the village women did.

Family Meetings

Many occasions provided a reason for a family meeting - the birth of a grandchild, the marriage of a niece or nephew, a pending discord between family members, the death anniversary or *cry die* of a relative who had died several years prior. During such gatherings, my grand aunts would come with some of their grandchildren. We would form a good playing team and play games like hide and seek, jumping on the squares, *awumbere* (singing and exchanging our hands in unison) and *echichi* (dancing and raising the same leg as the main dancer). We would spend long hours trying to eliminate each other at *echichi* dance. Sometimes, rice and stew were cooked for such occasions and everyone, especially the girls of the same age group would be given a big wooden bowl full of rice. With no cutlery, we would use our fingers to eat. Some of the greedy kids would carry very large portions of rice and swallow without even chewing a grain. When this happened, I would be so frustrated. I would sit back and watch them eat, completely baffled at the speed with which they ate. Sometimes, Ndih would encourage me to eat but I always found it difficult to partake in the hasty eating competition. When she and I were alone, she would remind me that this was the manner in which children who came from a large home normally ate. Coming from a large family, she said, children learned early on to fight for survival. Although I enjoyed playing with my cousins, I always looked forward to the end of these gatherings, exhausted from our games and frustrated by some of their eating habits. Some of them licked their fingers while they ate as if they were washing them with their own saliva! For many of the kids, these gatherings provided them with the rare opportunity to eat chicken, so they would move around with chicken parts - legs, heads and wings for hours – perhaps to show off to anyone that cared to know that they had just eaten chicken. By the way in some homes, children were prohibited from eating chickgen and eggs under the pretext that the children will become thieves.

14

VILLAGE FESTIVITIES

Christmas and New Year celebrations

Christmas was the favourite season among kids in Alah-tene. Relatives who worked in cities returned home for Christmas to spend the festive season with their family and often brought back bread, coconuts, sweets/candies and biscuits for kids. On Christmas eve, men and their wives, girls and boys gathered at the village square bars where they danced to "bottle dance" music. These performances were refereed by someone in the middle of the dance circle and his or her principal job was to eliminate those unable to follow the rhythm and instructions properly. People danced in pairs while we, the kids, would watch from outside through the windows. We derived much fun watching the dancers display their talents. The room was usually lit by a big Tilley lamp, and kerosene was added as needed to keep it aglow throughout the night. Watching some of the poor dancers, my friends and I swore we would do better when we became adults. However, before we could master the bottle dance moves, it faded out of popularity and was replaced by *high life, merengue* and *twist* dances.

Another popular Christmas activity was the masked dance fair organised by young children. Our group was made up of both girls and boys. Boys wore masks made of calabashes decorated in red and white and the girls sang a tune "Oh kokoriko, Ewah, oh kokoriko, ewah, Juju dong come, ewah," and some of the boys would respond "massa charge your pocket, sawa sawa never mind today". We would visit many homes across the village where we were given gifts of money for the dance or rice and stew. The boys would divide the money mostly amongst themselves and deceive the girls that some of it was missing. Nevertheless, it was always so much fun to be part of the Christmas kids' fanfare.

Alahtene inhabitants celebrated Christmas for a week by slaughtering pigs (pork stew and rice were the Christmas staple); then the feasting would move to New Year's celebration. Other popular dishes during this period included egusi pudding, achu, plantains and chicken. It was surprising to us that some people paid a lot of importance to New Year's Day celebrations. Many families would dress up in a common uniform on New Year's Day and take photographs. The photographer usually came from the city with his equipment which he treated with exceptional care. He would mount the camera, covered in black cloth on a high pole with two legs away from the family he was about to snap. When he was satisfied with the family's seating arrangement, he would return to his camera, peep under the dark cloth, then return to adjust people's heads, faces and mouths as needed. He would ask the children to remain quiet and to look straight at the direction of the camera. Many children feared the cameramen because they thought these men practiced magic with their equipment. This explains why many children cried when their photos were about to be snapped. Only a brave few smiled.

For many children, Christmas and New Year were the rare occasions when they got to put on new shoes. After the celebrations, the shoes were washed and safely kept for the next round of celebrations. However, parents often discovered with much regret that their children's feet had outgrown the shoes by the time the next big celebration presented itself.

Birth of a Child

The birth of a baby was a very happy occasion in Alahtene. All babies were delivered at home by local mid-wives. Women who had difficult pregnancies were often treated with herbs prescribed by an herbalist. The success rate of such treatments was remarkably high. Later, several ambulant mid-wives would visit the village and give a talk in church to pregnant women on the kinds of measures they needed to take to ensure they had healthy babies. They would also examine newborn babies to establish how healthy they were.

Some of the expecting mothers did not know the real names of their husbands, so when asked by the mid-wives, they would give the honorific "Tah or Tabue" which simply means father or father of such and such a child. This was fairly common if the women married husbands who already had other wives. Such men would normally be called "father of such and such a child", so the new wives would refer to their husbands in similar manner. Some young wives also thought it disrespectful to call their husbands by their given names.

Every kid always wanted to have a glimpse of a newborn baby. Some brave kids usually offered to carry the baby, while others, including me were afraid to carry newly born babies because they were so tender and delicate. I thought their limbs could easily break if they were not handled with care. As a result, I tended to carry toddlers only when they were creeping or walking. In homes with newly born babies, there was always plenty of cooked food for the new mother as well as for visitors.

As the number of babies increased, Christian parents began to organise collective christening ceremonies for their babies. These ceremonies were often followed by celebrations at the home of the parents of the baptised babies which were always attended by Sunday school children. There, they would be served sodas called "champagne", Grenadine, Fanta; sweet raffia or palm wine among others. Some of the sodas coloured our mouths red or yellow and we took pride in showing off our coloured tongues or lips especially to our mates who couldn't make it to the celebrations.

Marriages

Marriages between young people or older men marrying new wives was common. Wealthy men generally had at least four wives. Wealth by Alahtene's standards included having a large compound with several houses, plenty of farm-land, raffia palm bushes, goats, sheep, many wives and children. Some villagers were considered wealthy because they were direct descendants of the king. Marriage ceremonies provided opportunity for women to wear their colourful dresses, beads and head-ties.

When young men and women got married, the bride would be dressed in a loincloth that covered her breast and body. Her shoulder and face would be well anointed with palm oil and her hair braided with black thread. On the evening the bride was scheduled to be escorted to her husband's family home, she would be accompanied by friends and family and she would be anxiously awaited by the groom's family. The bridal party would walk slowly and advance multiple excuses as to why they couldn't increase their pace. Some of the excuses included the following: the bride's entourage was hungry, tired, their shoes hurt, or they needed drinks to quench their thirst from having walked a long way (even if the distance was just a few miles away). Gifts of money usually helped in accelerating the pace of the bridal party. As they walked, they would shower the bride with praises and sing of her astonishing beauty, how cultured she was; that she had been raised by such a beautiful family or village and that she keeps the company of good friends; her flat belly, flexible waist, etc.

The bride would beam with joy as her companions sang and praised her while they inched their way to the groom's home. Watching a bridal party was always an exciting event for us as children. Each of my friends had a unique aspect of the event they loved. Many loved the palm oil poured on the bride's body and some of us discussed that when we grow up, we would like to be anointed with palm oil as part of own marriage rites. However, that practice was soon replaced with camwood (a dry reddish powder obtained from grinding the bark of a special tree) much to the disappointment of those of us who preferred palm oil. Camwood gradually became a popular cosmetic which when used on the bride's body, resulted in a smooth, glowing texture.

After watching several of these marriage ceremonies, I asked Ndih why the bridal crowd always praised the bride's slim stomach. She explained that it was because the bride was not pregnant and that it was taboo for a bride to be pregnant before her wedding day.

One evening, a lady came to Ndih's house in tears and reported that her daughter had publicly disgraced her; she would become a laughingstock in the village – she said. The cause of her agony was because her daughter had fallen pregnant before her wedding day. How would she proceed with the wedding ceremony if her pregnancy showed? The aggrieved woman told Ndih that she had given lots of presents to other women's daughters and expected them to reciprocate when her daughter's turn came up. Ndih comforted the sobbing lady and advised her to arrange with the fiancé's family to speed up the marriage process. After the woman's departure, I asked Ndih why the lady was weeping. Ndih explained to me that the woman's daughter had dishonoured her by falling pregnant prior to her wedding ceremony. It puzzled me why this was considered disgraceful given that almost everyone loved children in Alahtene.

Prestige Titles

The king of Alahbukum recognised subjects for meritorious services or acts of bravery. These awards were titles of several types, grades and were normally conferred to individuals or groups during the king's annual dance or other special occasions. The titles were ranked and designated by specific insignia - red feathers, black feathers, bangles and caps, a woven bag with bells. The laureates were also always given a new name and exhorted to celebrate their accomplishments. It was customary for newly knighted individuals to celebrate their titles back in their villages of origin. To proceed, they would inform the council of elders and set a suitable date. Villagers would gather at the person's compound on the designated date where the village head would deliver a speech praising the recipient's title and the great honour it had brought to the village. Individuals who received these titles earned more respect and some even borrowed money to throw a feast to mark their new rank. The ceremonies usually ended with much eating, drinking and dancing.

The King's Annual Dance

A one-week feast held at the king's palace usually marked the end of the year in Alahbukum. This was known as *Abin e Mfor* - the king's annual dance. Each village in the kingdom composed and rehearsed their own songs and dance styles to be performed at the festival. The subjects of Alahtene selected through a competitive process, the song and dance they would perform at the king's annual dance. On each day of the festival, a specific village presented gifts to the king and performed their best dance. Figurines of carved statues and sculptures representing different ancestral gods or spirits were displayed by each of the dance groups. One of the most notable figurines was the *Maforti* which was believed to represent the soul of the fondom.

During the annual dance, the population feasted on their staple food - achu with yellow soup and drank palm or raffia wine. Ndih recounted that in her parents' time, a giant achu graced the festival; thousands of achu bundles were combined to form a massive mount and an equally sizeable hole was created in which the yellow soup was poured. Other items thrown into the giant meal included beef, dried fish, egusi pudding and garden eggs. Everyone ate from this giant achu as a symbol of unity among the people of Alahbukum.

The villages whose songs or dances were voted the best were awarded prizes. During the time spent with my grandmother,

Alahtene was awarded the top prize once. The festival usually attracted tourists who took many photographs. Villagers would display their titles, traditional attires and sing praises about the king who sat on his throne in the courtyard and watched the performances. Sometimes, he would descend from his throne and partake in the dancing. It was also common for Alahbukum subjects resident outside the kingdom to return home for the annual dance, during which they performed their own dances and paid allegiance to the king. It was also customary for neighbouring kings to attend the festival accompanied by their notables. Many believe that it was during these annual festivals that many young men met their future wives.

15

SAD EVENTS

Death

Death normally brought the entire village together especially when we learnt of the passing of an old man or woman. Upon hearing the news of someone's death, the elderly women would arrive at the home of the deceased, sit on the bare floor, mourn and call the name of the deceased, shower praises on the role the individual played and expressed how much the person would be missed, etc. Customary funeral dirges included eulogies that addressed the dead – one group would tune the solemn songs and the rest would answer in mournful tears. It was hard for anyone to listen to these mournful songs without shedding a tear. Children were not often allowed to see corpses.

One day, the village was shocked by the death of a kid of my age group called Nebong. The pretty little girl fell sick for three days only and died. She had complained of severe headache and fever after school and all the herbs administered to her did not help. Her corpse was washed, dressed in a little white gown and white powder applied on her face. Her body was then laid on a bed in one of the rooms in her parents' home. Kids of her age group were allowed to get into the room to see her body. I went in, looked at her still and peaceful corpse, and she looked like she was smiling in her sleep. I wondered why it was said she was dead. "She was not breathing" my other age mates later told me. Her relatives were wailing in the yard and moved by the pain of their loss, we joined them in weeping. That was my first encounter with the dead and it stuck in my memory till this day. Perhaps the kid may have suffered from meningitis.

Not long after Nebong's death, a team of public health personnel came from the capital city to vaccinate all children against a deadly disease called meningitis. In school, pupils lined up with frightened eyes on the designated date and spot, scared to death of the needles. Each child received the shot on the left arm or shoulder and many cried due to the pain of the needle. Some kids who were terrified of needles would come close to the vaccination team's table and then run off to the tail of the line in panic. They were either scared of dying like Nebong or the anticipated pain from the vaccination. Although the vaccines made some kids to develop a fever the next day, none of the kids of my age group ever died again from what we believed was meningitis. Later in life, we learned that we were very fortunate not to have contracted the disease after visiting the corpse of our late friend. In those days, infectious diseases like meningitis were prevalent during the dry seasons.

Deworming of Kids

A "children's deworming" exercise used to be conducted during my time in Alahtene. The medication was brought from the hospital in the city and administered to kids very early in the morning. On the set season and date, children, five and above would be awoken early in the morning to be administered the designated worm medicine. All eligible children would assemble at the village market square. A large wooden table containing several big bottles of liquid medication would be placed in front of the medical personnel. Each kid would be given two tablespoonsful of the liquid made from castor oil – a slimy liquid without any sugar and awful in odour. It was forced into our mouths, down into our throats with our nostrils tightly held together. A waiting supervisor held a cane and watched closely to whip any child who tried to vomit the medication. After taking the medication, we were deprived of food and water and only ate a ripe banana around noon. By two o'clock in the afternoon, the worms started coming out. Children excreted so many worms in their stool so much so that the medical personnel lost count.

For the young children, the de-worming exercise was one of their worst medical treatments, besides the meningitis vaccination. Kids hated taking the worm medicine although it made a huge difference in their health. As a result of their treatment, they became healthy eaters of both fruits and food; their big stomachs, possibly inflated by worms reduced significantly. Furthermore, it became rare to see children whose nostrils oozed worms as the case had been prior to the treatment. This new modern treatment eventually replaced the traditional slimy liquid obtained from a plant called *nkwore (slimy plant)* with which grandmother had once treated me without success.

When I look back at that period, I now understand why many children in Alahtene were afflicted by worms; it was due to the general lack of hygienic behaviours; children ate without washing their hands; ate unwashed fruits, drank polluted water and walked around barefooted, etc.

The Village Mad Man

Mah Ngwebancho had an only brother who had gone to work in the coastal plantations. His name was Tah Nagwah, a tall handsome man who always had a broad smile on his face. As a young man he and his friends had also trekked for a week to the coastal town where the colonial masters had established the banana, tea and rubber plantations. Their ambition was to find work, learn the modern way of life, save enough money to pay the required bride price for their wives, build a house and start a family. He worked hard, earned some money, bought a radio and snapped a photograph of himself, dressed in a white shirt, a pair of trousers, tie, black shoes, well-trimmed haircut and a broad smile on his handsome face. The photo showed him in front of a house roofed with corrugated iron sheets, holding the radio set in his hand lifted towards his ear as a sign of achievement. He sent the photo home to his elder sister in the village which was used to search for a beautiful bride for him. Ndih and her three friends used the man's photo to woo Ndag Nchang, one of the most beautiful girls at the time in the village and to request her hand in marriage.

The young lady was so delighted with the young man's looks and achievements, so she accepted the marriage proposal. A photograph of Ndag Nchang was also sent to Nagwah. He happily sent money for the bride price and all customary preparations were done including the demands made by Ndag Nchang and her family. What was left was for Nagwah to return to the village and welcome his new bride on the scheduled wedding day, following which the three-day feasting would take place. While he worked hard, trying to save as much money as possible, another young man arrived from nowhere, out of the blue and began courting the village belle. Some people spotted them together at unusual hours and expressed concern.

One early morning, the bride's parents woke up and discovered that she had vanished, leaving no trace behind. Before long, they figured out that she had eloped with the new suitor. Her mother wept profusely as if her daughter were dead. Her husband blamed her mother for not having given their daughter sufficient maternal advice. He told his wife to find the money to reimburse the bride price already paid by prince Nagwah or he would abandon her and her other daughters and seek refuge somewhere else.

Distraught by the turn of events, Ndag Nchang's mother came with a sad face to Ndih's house one early morning and burst into tears. How would she face Ndih's friend, Mah Ngwebancho, a princess for that matter, the elder sister to prince Nagwah? She decried the fact that Ndag Nchang had brought shame on her and that as her first daughter, her elopement would bring bad luck to her other daughters. Ndih comforted the sad woman and suggested that she and her husband should brainstorm on how to reimburse the bride price instead of blaming each other. News of the elopement spread like wildfire throughout the village and coincided with the arrival of a letter from Nagwah in which he announced the intended date of their wedding - the day after the market day, a month from the date of the reception of the letter.

Nagwah finally arrived in the village and lodged at his sister's home. People visited him as custom demanded. Women brought food while the men brought raffia palm wine and akwacha. Nagwah had brought some smulgri, the most popular beer of the day, smuggled from the neighbouring country. He also brought Kronenbourg, a colonial beer which many people had boycotted after independence in protest to colonial rule.

Tah Kereti, the village gossiper also came to visit. He sat next to Nagwah, itchy to break the bad news about the elopement. Those who were around gave him a stern look, hoping to deter him from breaking the news. After gulping down a bottle of smulgri, he smiled in an uncomfortable manner, whispered something to the newcomer, and right then, everyone knew he had done the dreadful thing – this, because Nagwah's countenance changed automatically. He called a few persons around the room to confirm the bad news and many with solemn faces asked him to be strong and to endure the sad situation. Nagwah held himself together for a while as the celebrations to welcome him continued late into the night until he started to behave in an odd manner. Many people thought he was drunk but the next day his condition worsened. He had gone mad with rage as a result of losing his fiancée for whom he had paid a hefty bride price. He believed the entire village had conspired against him and had withheld the truth from him. How come nobody had informed him of the fact that his fiancée had eloped? He began insulting everybody and gradually became violent. He moved about with a big club in his hand and chased adults, children and even attacked passers-by. Reacting to his erratic behaviour, the bigger boys started calling him "mad man" – a label that made him even more violent. Eventually, the village elders held a council meeting and decided that Nagwah ought to be put in fetters and demanded that his family should take him to a traditional doctor for treatment.

Ndih's friend Mah Ngwebancho, Nagwah's only sister, had long escaped from her home to the farm where her son lived. Her grandson too had abandoned the compound and returned to his parent's home. The "mad man" was now abandoned to himself in Tah Nujala's home. He would spend hours talking to himself, cursing all the villagers and calling them wicked creatures. He barely had any food to eat and grew thinner. He disliked children's voices, so, when we went to fetch water and had to pass by the house where he lodged, we would tiptoe as best as we could. Every now and then he would visit Ndih's house in search of food. Ndih would serve him food and while he ate, she would ask why he behaved like a mad man. He would respond that he felt the village was attacking him ever since he came back home; he would say every cent he had worked had been paid as bride price for his eloped fiancée. I would stick around and pretend as if I were not staring at him, because he hated being stared at. Nagwah made life unliveable for many residents, some of whom decided to abandon their homes and sought refuge in other villages or their farms. The heavy wooden fetters that were intended to restrain him didn't seem to work. He would still beat up people, throw spears at them and move about bearing dangerous weapons likes knives. With time, his condition deteriorated and the worst came when he burnt down Ndag Nchang's father's thatched house which prompted the composition of a song called *Ndag Nchang ooh.*

Eventually, the council of elders sent a messenger to the city to report to the *jahs* about the situation in Alahtene. A few days later, a team of law enforcement officers arrived in a Land rover vehicle and took Tah Abarah (the mad man's new name) to jail in the big city. After spending a few days in jail, he returned home seemingly cured and without the fetters. However, not long after he settled in, the illness re-afflicted him.

One day, my friend and I were on our way to fetch water at the stream and we tiptoed outside his house as we normally did.

Unfortunately for us, he overheard our footsteps and immediately stormed outside and began to chase us. We ran and screamed my grandmother's name as I sought refuge inside her house. My friend also ran as fast as an antelope to her parents' home. The mad man pursued me to my grandmother's house and stood at the door panting and pointing his spear at me, admonishing us never to pass by his residence again. My grandmother yelled back and instructed him to take his madness elsewhere and that he should refrain from harassing her granddaughter.

Coincidentally, my father came visiting the next day. He heard the news about our narrow escape from the menacing mad man, so he decided to visit the man early the next morning. He questioned the mad man why he had threatened to kill us, and the latter denied any intentions of having done such a thing. Angered by the man's response, dad pulled out a cane he had brought along and began to whip the mad man who stormed out and began to run towards the road that led to the city. Other men heard the commotion and joined the chase to catch him, but he outpaced them and eventually arrived in the city. He ended up locating the house of one of his maternal uncles from where he was immediately taken for treatment. He spent a few months with a traditional doctor who specialised in treating mental illness and news was sent to Alahtene that he had been completely healed.

Tah Nagwah's maternal grand uncle was the king of Alahmanku, a neighbouring village. When the king learnt that his grandnephew had returned from treatment and had no property or house to call his own, he ordered that several acres of land should be given to his grandnephew. Tah Nagwah moved to Alahmanku where he built himself a good house, married three beautiful wives and fathered several children. He and his wives and children cultivated the fertile land and he became a rich farmer. He had long forgotten about Ndag Nchang!

Many years after he had settled in his grandfather's kingdom, Tah Nagwah paid a visit to Alahtene, coincidentally on the market day. The crowd at the market was overjoyed when they realised he was the former mad man and his visit soon turned into a celebration. He ordered food and drinks for everyone present - corn beer, akwacha, palm wine, smulgri, puff puff, akara, fried fish and suya.

When he visited Ndih to tell of his good fortune, Ndih reminded him that many sick people had died due to negligence from their relatives. She suggested that if Nagwah had not moved to his mother's relatives, he would have died from hunger and the lack of love. Before leaving, he showered Ndih with gifts. Ndih later told me after the man had gone that Nagwah had been lucky to find his relatives in the city. Had he gone instead to the marketplace stark naked, Ndih said, he would never have been cured – based on their commonly held beliefs.

Until his death at an old age, Tah Nagwah never ceased to be grateful that he left Alahtene to reunite with his kinsmen in Alahmanku.

Murder in the Village

Citizens of Alahtene woke up one early morning to the shocking news of the murder of one of theirs during the night. The incident occurred on a *Mbindoh*, the customary market day which was usually characterised by merrymaking. The victim was a young handsome man with a beautiful wife and child. Tah Numbang had been happily married for less than three years. He and his young family lived in a compound with his elder brother who had a wife and four children. Their compound had four houses built in a rectangular manner. As was customary, each brother had his own separate living quarters while their wives and children had their own living quarters.

All of them had visited the market on that fateful day but the women had returned home before their husbands. Tah Numbang had stayed even longer in the market, drinking akwacha and recounting stories with friends. His brother was also at another pub where he spent his time dancing and drinking with his own friends. By the time Tah Numbang got home, it was pitch dark and his murderer was hiding somewhere near his house awaiting his return. The brothers' wives were preparing dinner in their respective houses while their children had gathered at the older brother's wife's house, telling stories and waiting for the evening meal. Mrs Numbang was cooking and cheerfully singing, remembering how happy things had been at the market where she had spent the day with her husband.

Tah Numbang arrived home singing, as it was customary for men to sing to announce their arrival or to scare off any intruder. While cooking corn fufu and njama-njama, she heard her husband scream – "Oh I'm dead! Oh, I'm dead!" - a sudden change from his singing just a short moment prior. She listened keenly again and heard her husband's screams and call for help. She collected her lamp and rushed in the direction of the screams and as she approached her husband, she saw the silhouette of a tall heavily built man running away into the dark night. Her husband was on the ground, groaning in pain and pointed weakly to the spot where he had been stabbed. The other brother's wife stormed out of her house to help. It was then that they noticed Tah Numbang was bleeding profusely from his heart, so they screamed at the top of their voices and neighbours rushed to the scene. A neighbour rushed back to his house to bring a bicycle for them to transport Tah Numbang to the nearest hospital, about fifteen miles away. By the time the neighbour got back a few minutes later, it was too late; Tah Numbang had passed away, leaving everyone in profound shock. No one could recall the last time such a hideous crime had happened in Alahtene.

The murderer had disappeared into the dark night with no one unable to identify him. The next morning, the whole village gathered in shock at the victim's home as the news continued to spread like wildfire. The council of elders reported the matter first to the police in town and secondly to the king of Alahbukum. Two police officers came and took statements from the women and neighbours. They also snapped photographs of the victim and assured everyone that the murderer would be caught. The villagers believed the policemen because the latter had claimed that their cameras could reveal the identity of the suspect by carefully looking at the victim's eyes. Meanwhile, the king sent a top member of the much-dreaded regulatory society known as *kwifor* to "spoil Tah Numbang's corpse" – that is, to perform certain rituals over his body. It was believed that if properly carried out, the ritual would cause the murderer to fall sick and would be unable to die without confessing to their crime.

After Tah Numbang's funeral, the council of elders launched a manhunt for the murderer, but the search yielded nothing. Some people suspected that the murderer may have been part of the search team. Others suspected the Fulani herdsmen in the neighbouring village but this was quickly dismissed because no one could attest to any business between the murdered man and Fulani herdsmen. Tah Numbang's murder was even more puzzling because he had no apparent problems or enemies known to anyone in the village.

Shortly after Tah Numbang's funeral rites, rumour started circulating about a huge man who allegedly had been seen many times talking to the late man's wife at dusk. The rumours were proven true when the man married Tah Numbang's widow. However, people were terrified to speak out because this man, Tah Atutu had replaced the deceased as a member of the village council of elders. People consoled themselves by claiming that if the rituals were to be trusted, the suspect, Tah Atutu would confess his deeds before dying.

As I grew up and reflected on Tah Numbang's murder, which as far as I could remember, was the first unsolved murder mystery in the history of Alahtene, I blamed the failure to catch Tah Numbang's murderer to the lack of electricity in the village. Perhaps if there was electricity in his compound, the murder would not have occurred in the first place – so I thought. However, I also remembered that elsewhere, people are murdered in broad daylight or in well-lit buildings. I also pondered about the police claims that their camera could help to identify the murderer by carefully examining the victim's eyes. Perhaps, the police had suggested this theory to serve as a deterrence to potential criminals. But if their theory were true, how would they go about it when Tah Numbang's murder happened at night? Is there any chance he saw his murderer in that pitch dark night? Eventually, the police report did not reveal Tah Numbang's murderer, like thousands of other unsolved murders in the country.

Tah Atutu married and eventually had four children with Numbang's widow. He was also eventually stricken by a mysterious disease and no amount of traditional medicine could bring him relief. His health continued to deteriorate as he remained bed-ridden, barely conscious of his surroundings. One day when one of his friends from the village council visited, he asked him to invite the council head to see him because he had a confession to make. When the council head arrived, he confessed to Numbang's murder, an incident that was witnessed by a small crowd. This confirmed a wise saying in Alahtene that "karma takes time, but it always happens". Although I learnt of this confession, I resolved that I would study law and hopefully become a lawyer, judge or police commissioner in the future so that I could solve murder cases like Tah Numbang's.

Every now and then, someone died suddenly in Alahtene, having been sick for just a few days. Some people believed that these sudden deaths were because of poisoning. A few deaths were recorded of individuals who played the drums all night long during festivities; upon returning home, they vomited and died. From my enquiry with medical professionals later in life, most of them suggested that these sudden deaths might have been cases of heart attacks or hypertension from the overconsumption of fatty foods, carbohydrates, excessive consumption of wildlife beef and heavy drinking of smulgri, akwacha, nkang, locally brewed whisky, etc. hernia, diabetes, or malaria. Although traditional medicine then was effective, many people hardly visited the lone hospital for appropriate medical check-up because it was located many miles away. It was also common for locals if they saw someone taking their medications, to ask if that person could share their medication. If you pressed the person begging for medicine if they knew what the medicine was meant to cure, they would say,

"I have so many sicknesses in my body ranging from body pains to everything, so if I take part of that medication, it will obviously cure me." Everybody shared medications with each other especially a popular pain killer called "Mambi". When I grew up, I found out that its actual name was "M&B".

16

STRANGERS

Herdsmen from the Hills

Up on the hilltop by the entrance to Alahtene, from the direction of the town market road, there lived several herdsmen with their families. Their settlement was between Alahtene and Njienki and their main occupation was cattle and sheep rearing. Known as the Bororo people, they used to be nomads until the king of Alahbukum gave them a large piece of land on the hill tops. Their houses were made of grass round huts and their staple meal was corn fufu with meat stew or vegetable. Each family had at least three large huts in a compound, and it was rumoured that they always abandoned their village upon the death of their chief, known as the Ardo. The main animals they herded were cattle, sheep and poultry. Children normally inherited them from their parents. Cattle and sheep were also the favoured items when paying the bride price for a new wife according to their custom.

Their chief was called Ardo Jiggama and their village was named after him. He had many wives and children. One of his wives and the most trusted was called Mama Abakwa. Ardo Jiggama and some of his princes rode on horsebacks wherever they went and especially when they were looking after their herds. They had a different culture from ours, spoke a different language which could be understood by their kinsmen spread all over West Africa. They had three major ceremonies: marriages, end of fasting (Ramadan) and rites of passage for boys as they transitioned into men. During their marriage ceremonies, the bride and bridegroom would dress colourfully, dance together on the main road to the rhythm of tambourines, huge drums and long bamboo flutes and the cheering crowd of women and children. After the public dancing which lasted several hours, feasting would continue at the new couple's compound. Celebrations entailed an abundance of roasted beef, rice, cassava and fried ripe plantains.

At the end of Ramadan, the Ardo would ride a decorated horse accompanied by many of his male subjects on their own decorated horses. If the Ardo stopped somewhere, his subjects would sprint their horses and stop abruptly at the spot where the Ardo's horse stood. His subjects would then raise their spears up into the air, chant praises to the Ardo and salute him with extravagant titles. During the boys' rites of passage, they would dance slowly, singing sacred songs. The young kids from Alahtene who often watched these ceremonies from the sidelines would repeat the songs throughout the year with much fanfare.

Ardo Jiggama and his family were my dad's friends and they frequently visited Ndih especially on local market days. They would ask about my father each time they visited. The women from Ardo's village sold milk, kurukuru, akara banana, and poultry. The men on the other hand were mostly butchers and also sold live sheep, goats and cattle. The heart of every slaughtered cow on the local market day was sent to the king of Alahbukum as tribute and as a sign of Ardo Jiggama's allegiance to him. More than ten cows were killed on a weekly basis for the Alahtene market by the Ardo's men.

Bororo women frequently brought fresh cow milk for Ndih and in turn, Ndih gave them dry corn, cassava and sometimes sweet potatoes. Ndih did not like fresh milk, so I drank a lot of it because my uncle Ajuenekoh was frequently away from the house either running chores or playing with his friends. Ndih would express appreciation to them for their gift so much so that they thought Ndih loved raw milk. Although she did not drink it, she said it was good for my health. I also made many trips to the hilltop village to collect fresh milk and give foodstuff from Ndih to her Bororo friends – especially if a week had gone by without her hearing from them. I was always terrified by the bellowing of their cows, especially when they stared at me with their threatening eyes. I thought they might bite or thrust me into the air with their horns. Mami Damendab, Ardo's first wife would invite me to walk among the herd of animals, reassuring me that cows do not bite. I often obliged and would walk through the herd, sweating with fright.

Before taking the cows to the slaughterhouse, their neck and legs would be tied with ropes – a process they resisted forcefully. Each cow was led by two men; the person in front held the rope fastened on its neck and a second man held the rope tied to the animal's leg. Should the enraged cow resist to move, the man at the back would pull the ropes, prompting the miserable animal to move. Today, when I recall these memories, it seems the cows always knew that once the ropes were tied on their neck and feet, they were heading on a journey of no return, thus prompting them to fight back.

The slaughterhouse in Alahtene was located about five hundred metres from the market. It had a large slab housed within a structure of four high pillars and a thatched grass roof. Blood from the slaughtered animals was channelled to a pit although people frequently collected the flowing blood to boil for their dog's food. Cow horns were thrown all over the slaughterhouse and craftsmen would pick them up for decoration and resale. Behind the slaughterhouse, flies feasted on a pile of excrement and disposed parts from the slaughtered animals.

Years later, when I worked to develop environmentally friendly policies for my country, I visited a slaughterhouse in Botswana, managed by the country's meat commission. They slaughtered one thousand two hundred cows per day and every part of the animal was used; their hair was used for making fake fur coats and wigs, the horns were used to make buttons, their leg bones for making heels for women's shoes, their blood was collected by the lipstick industry, and their excrement were used to prepare fertilizer. I found their production system highly industrialised and efficient which explained why a significant portion of their beef was exported to the European Union.

I looked back and remembered with regret how these materials were wasted in Alahtene; how Alahtene's little slaughterhouse had declined over the years, especially after wealthy buyers from the neighbouring country came and bought most of the cattle left behind by Ardo Jiggama to his misguided heirs.

The Village White Women

Ndih's elder sister lived in a distant village, Ntah Akareh near Alahbukum's capital, about three hour's trek from

Alahtene. One day, she fell sick and when the news reached Ndih Maghrebong, she decided to visit her sick sister. I carried a basket of cooked food on my head and Ndih braved the long journey despite her poor eyesight. It was in Ntah Akareh that early protestant missionaries had constructed a health centre. There, more and more women came to deliver their babies; children were brought to be treated for various diseases, and other people were treated for snake bites, malaria, accidents etc. Complicated medical cases were referred to the lone hospital in the city several miles away.

As we drew nearer to the health centre, three white women stood outside conversing in English. Ndih greeted them in Befue, the name of our language. They all answered and inquired where Ndih was heading to. They also asked what my name was and I responded - Nasi. Ndih told them I was her granddaughter and that we were on our way to visit her sick sister. The three women instructed Ndih to bring her sister to the health centre if she found her still sick. I was quite baffled by the white women's ability to speak our language fluently. I was also lost in admiration of the health centre's beautiful buildings made of baked bricks – hence its name "Ntah Akareh" which meant the Whiteman's Hill.

The three missionaries had lived among the villagers for many years and participated in all their activities. It was thanks to this that they communicated fluently in the local language, ate our food and danced so well to our traditional music. While I was lost in my admiration of the three ladies and the beautiful buildings, Ndih continued walking and only realised after a long distance that I had not been following her, that I had been lost in a reverie admiring the beautiful buildings, so she called out. When I caught up with her after running as fast as I could with the food basket on my head, I told her that when I grew up, I would build my house to resemble the health centre buildings. Ndih applauded my idea and said the sky was my limit.

17

BAD WEATHER AND NDIH'S BRAVERY

Rainstorms and heavy winds were major threats to all residents of Alahtene. Stormy weather usually destroyed plantain stems, fruit trees and many crops such as corn and beans. Rainstorms always flooded the streams and kids were warned to avoid streams during such storms.

Notables usually carried out an annual appeasement rite inside a small bamboo hut with thatched roof located at the market square. The hut was known as *Ndah Takumbeng*. They would cut various species of grass and mix them with certain liquids, including chicken blood while chanting solemn ritual songs. This rite was intended to appease the gods and to solicit their protection from the ravages of the stormy weather.

When the heavy rains were accompanied with hailstones, excited kids would go about running in the rain, collecting hailstones and sucking them. We loved playing in the rain and enjoyed showering in it for several hours. Eventually, we would become cold and then retreat into the house shivering, desperate for the warmth of the fireside.

Despite the appeasement rites, the storms were always

intense - roof tops would be blown off, huge eucalyptus trees brought down, bridges swept away, and sometimes, little kids got drown. It was a popular belief that the storm usually arose from a big river, "Mbiih" - the palace of the king of the gods who always went on an annual journey with a huge delegation of his subjects. Some people claimed that during the passage of the "king of the gods", his subjects would play drums and flutes, sing songs, and push down anything on his path like houses, huge trees, stone objects, etc. Sometimes the storms would be accompanied by lightning and thunder, striking grazing cows on the hills and even humans.

During such stormy weather, Ndih would meditate, say a prayer and talk to the weather saying "I'm an innocent widow, I live in this house here alone with my children, I have never been envious of anybody or their children; I have never stolen or taken someone's property falsely; you this storm, lightning and thunder, just go to where you are heading, you cannot stop at my door as I neither know nor owe you; if you look through my house your eyes will be blinded, just keep going; I give food to the hungry and I am sure I have fed even some of your own people and children, keep going where you are heading to." I would listen to her speech which I thought was a melodrama. I would ask Ndih "with whom are you talking?" and she would sigh and answer in a melancholic tone "I am speaking to the storm". The storms always spared Ndih's house except for minor damage to tall corn in the garden around her compound. Once, it rained hailstones which remained on the ground for more than a day and made the whole environment very cold. Later in life, I reckoned that the huge eucalyptus trees and fruit trees that surrounded Manghrebong's house played a major role in mitigating the impact of the storms on her home. While other people's homes got destroyed, Ndih's always stood unscathed. Perhaps, it was also because of her faith that her home was always spared.

GLOSSARY OF TERMS

Ndih - an honorific used to address old or senior women.

Tah - a word mostly used by children to address their dads; it is also the English equivalent of mister, sir.

Tahgha - one's father

Mah - the short form of Magha, an honorific when addressing the king's wives; also extended to elderly princesses in Alahtene.

Befue - the language spoken by the Bafut people of the Cameroon Grasssfields.

Alahtene - Fictitious name for a place where people survive for the most part without the comforts of modern life.

Mooh - an honorific used to address princes and princesses in Alahtene

Smulgri - term used to designate any contraband or smuggled goods especially beer. In this novel, it is used to describe the various imported beers for which duties ought to be paid but locals smuggled them through the porous borders. It is likely derived from the English word, smuggled.

Akwacha - a local beer produced from fermented and germinating corn. The drink is thick and creamy in colour.

Nkang - A local beer prepared from fermented and fried corn. It is sweet when freshly produced and brownish in colour, like a Guinness stout. It becomes alcoholic after a few days of further fermentation.

Champagne - a type of soda, light yellowish in colour and was popular during the early 1960s. It disappeared from the market by the mid-1960s.

Ntah Akareh - The Whiteman's Hill; the name of a suburb, so-called because the first missionaries settled that area.

Jahs - the term used to describe gendarmes

SIGNS, WISE SAYINGS AND COMMON ALAHTENE PROVERBS

1. While you care for someone's child, even your sibling's, you should also deliver yours.
2. If you are waiting for someone, you should keep moving or carry on with your chores because certain persons would keep you waiting indefinitely.
3. *The young animal follows its mother's footsteps*; that is, like mother, like daughter.
4. *A young animal eats the same type of herbs its mother eats*; that is, children imitate what their parents do (good and bad).
5. *When an animal is old, it sucks the breast of its young ones*; that is, an old person depends on his or her children's care.
6. *Nobody should be watching or scrutinizing the hands that weeds the farm or those of someone sharing palm oil*; this means that those who are involved in implementing a gainful activity should always benefit from it without being closely watched.
7. *Brothers or siblings fight using only their elbows, they don't inflict lethal blows on each other*; this means that siblings should not inflict each other serious injuries or insults in a conflict even when one is wrong.

8. *A baby does not survive long in a house where there is constant bickering;* this means that where family members are constantly quarrelling among themselves, such a home would not experience good fortune.

9. *An animal which does not listen to the jingling of the hunting dogs' bells is doomed to be caught by the hunter;* it means that any person who does not listen to advice is destined for destruction.

10. *A river meanders through valleys and forests because there is nobody to advise it to flow straight;* this means that those who take to advice attain their goals within a record time.

11. *An obedient child even in a foreign land can succeed the king of that land;* this means that obedience, hard work and humility rewards greatly.

12. *A fly which heeds no advice finally ends up buried in the grave with the corpse;* a person who does not see the signs of danger, or heed to advice would end up in doom.

13. *A heady child who does not heed the advice of his or her parents will always lose his blessings.*

14. *Although a monkey's tail is so long and heavy, it still carries it along conveniently;* this means that a person should never throw away a bad child under the pretext that it is bad; always develop a way to cope with a bad situation with joy.

15. *A child who has gone through the heart of an elephant;* this refers to a child who is brave to a fault or too daring.

16. *Everybody has their heads on their necks;* this means that everyone bears consequences for their acts, including children.

17. *The shoulder can never grow above the head;* this means that an elder is always the wiser person even if he or she

grows old.

18. *To put a hot stone in a child's pocket until the child plunges into the river to cool him/herself;* this means to punish a child so severely until he/she never repeats the same bad act in future.

19. In Ndih's days, the people of Alahtene had signs which they interpreted as signifying good or ill fortune. For instance, if owls hooted at night near someone's house or on their roof top, it was interpreted that witches were visiting or that a death would occur within the family.

20. If cats continuously meowed, purred, growled, or hissed at night behind somebody's house, it was a sign of ill omen.

21. If someone was walking and dashed his/her left foot on a stone, it meant his/her mission would be unfruitful. If someone was on a journey and an animal crossed the road from right to left, it meant the journey or mission would be fruitful.

22. If somebody's upper eye lid twitched several times, it meant he or she would welcome a stranger or cry (depending on whether it was one's right or left eye lid). If one's right hand shook involuntarily several times, it meant one would receive money or a good gift from someone.

23. Locusts which eat one another - this refers to a self destructive family, group, community, society or nation.

ACKNOWLEDGEMENT

Although this novel is fictional, it is inspired by true events in the life of an extraordinary woman, my grandmother, Ndih Manghrebong, from the time her grandchild Sibi started living with her. She impacted the lives of many people in Alahtene in many positive ways. Ndih was an embodiment of love, truth, honesty, and hard work. She had so much positive energy with which she empowered many women and was an inspiration to other members of the community. Her high sense of justice made her uncomfortable to work with the village head who was also the head of the council of elders – an institution that had become notoriously corrupt.

Her house became a day care centre and home to many kids who lacked proper care in their own parents' houses. She would shower the children with love and encourage even the intellectually weak ones to unlock their potentials. Unlike most mothers back then, she refused to call any child negative names, thereby nurturing confidence in the young children; she also promoted excellence among young people and women. Every child learned to do at least one useful little thing because of Ndih's encouragements. Many kids returned to their parents completely transformed. Some mothers would ask Ndih what she did for their children to carry out certain tasks; Ndih would simply tell them; "some children need patience to learn while others need love and competition".

She would advise and encourage young women to have other multiple income-generating activities in order not to depend solely on their husbands as was the custom in those days.

The adventures of her granddaughter growing up in her care at Alahtene reveal her subtle role in moulding not only her progeny but all the other kids who were attracted to her abode.

Her epitaph should have read something like this: "Here lies a workaholic, a great woman of value who was an inspiration to many, a woman who lived ahead of her times". Although she had no tombstone, her good deeds are inscribed in our hearts forever.

My special gratitude also goes to my mentor Dr Niba Matthias Livinus whose invaluable advice enabled me to complete the manuscript and directed me to the publisher at Spears Books. You devoted hours reading over the initial drafts and provided invaluable corrections. Sadly, you exited this world before the novel's publication. Without your input, this work would have been gathering dust on my shelf. I will forever remain indebted to your friendship and support.

I thank my grandson, Nathan, my niece, Peace, who individually read early drafts of this book and were so delighted with all the stories therein. They said it will be every young person's must-read novel.

Gratitude also goes to Prof Jude Fokwang who edited several drafts of this work. You are deeply appreciated. A huge thanks to everyone on my publishing team, including Toh Bright for designing the beautiful cover artwork.

Mary S. Fosi © Photo credit, Author

Mary S. Fosi is an environmental Consultant and Chairperson of the *Myrianthus Fosi Foundation for Biodiversity and Environmental Protection* (MyFF), a Non-Governmental Organization that provides public awareness on environmental issues to local communities for improved sustainable livelihoods. She started her career in 1974 in the Cameroon public service, serving in the Ministries of Social and Women's Affairs, the Administrative Bench of the Supreme Court, the Ministry of Environment and Forestry and the Ministry of Environment and Nature Protection. She occupied positions of responsibility including as Chief of Service, Director and Technical Adviser. She coordinated projects funded by the World Bank, the Global Environment Facility and UNEP, and headed government missions to various international negotiations on the environment and forestry issues. She represented Cameroon within the African Ministerial Council on the Environment

(AMCEN); International Compliance Committee of the Cartagena Protocol on Biosafety; Bureau of the Conference of Parties to the Convention on Biodiversity; Member of the Conference of Central African Ministers on Forestry (COMIFAC) and AAPAM Bureau. She retired in 2009 and has since then, served as a consultant to the FAO, UNEP, UNIDO, UNESCO and GTZ.

MyFF was created in 2011 in commemoration of the Award conferred on her by the Royal Kew Botanical Gardens, London, naming a plant species - *myrianthus fosi* after her in recognition of her immense contribution to biodiversity conservation and environmental protection. She has reviewed many professional articles and conference proceedings on the environment, published in environmental/scientific journals and co-authored a book on biosafety. *Sibi's Adventures in Alahtene* is her first novel.

Mary holds a Degree in Law from the University of Yaounde, and a Higher Diploma from the School of Administration and Magistracy (ENAM), Cameroon. She now lives in the USA with her children.

Meet Sibi, a vivacious, smart, and audacious girl who leaves the comforts of her coastal town and parents to live with Ndih, her granny in the village of Alahtene. Sibi's integration into village life is swift and adventurous, aided by the ever-soothing supervision of her equally gallant grandmother and teenage uncle, Ajuenekoh. Recounted from the first person, we follow Sibi's adventures in school, church, neighbourhoods, the rivers, hills and forests of Alahtene, its buzzy market and most significantly, around Ndih's fireside. Set in the early 1960s, *Sibi's Adventures in Alahtene* bubbles with dozens of breathtaking stories about the intrigues of adult life as much as about childhood in a rural community rapidly integrating into a newly formed African country.

ABOUT THE PUBLISHER

Spears Books is an independent publisher dedicated to providing innovative publication strategies with emphasis on African/Africana stories and perspectives. As a platform for alternative voices, we prioritize the accessibility and affordability of our titles in order to ensure that relevant and often marginal voices are represented at the global marketplace of ideas. Our titles – poetry, fiction, narrative nonfiction, memoirs, reference, travel writing, African languages, and young people's literature – aim to bring African worldviews closer to diverse readers. Our titles are distributed in paperback and electronic formats globally by African Books Collective.

Connect with Us: Go to www.spearsmedia.com to learn about exclusive previews and read excerpts of new books, find detailed information on our titles, authors, subject area books, and special discounts.

Subscribe to our Free Newsletter: Be amongst the first to hear about our newest publications, special discount offers, news about bestsellers, author interviews, coupons and more! Subscribe to our newsletter by visiting www.spearsmedia.com

Quantity Discounts: Spears Books are available at quantity discounts for orders of ten or more copies. Contact Spears Books at orders@spearsmedia.com.

Host a Reading Group: Learn more about how to host a reading group on our website at www.spearsmedia.com

Printed in the United States
by Baker & Taylor Publisher Services